Love Enough for Two

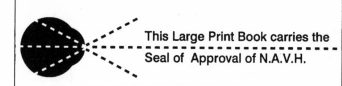

This Large Print Book carries the
Seal of Approval of N.A.V.H.

Love Enough for Two

Cynthia Rutledge

Thorndike Press • Waterville, Maine

Copyright © 2004 by Cynthia Rutledge

Published in 2005 by arrangement with Harlequin Books S.A.

Thorndike Press® Large Print Romance.

The tree indicium is a trademark of Thorndike Press.

The text of this Large Print edition is unabridged. Other aspects of the book may vary from the original edition.

Set in 16 pt. Plantin by Myrna S. Raven.

Printed in the United States on permanent paper.

Library of Congress Cataloging-in-Publication Data

Rutledge, Cynthia.
    Love enough for two / Cynthia Rutledge.
        p. cm.
    ISBN 0-7862-7226-0 (lg. print : hc : alk. paper)
    1. Single mothers — Fiction.   2. Mothers and daughters — Fiction.   3. Large type books.   I. Title.
PS3618.U825L68 2005
813´.6—dc22   2004061507

To my wonderful daughter, Wendy

National Association for Visually Handicapped
serving the partially seeing

As the Founder/CEO of NAVH, the only national health agency solely devoted to those who, although not totally blind, have an eye disease which could lead to serious visual impairment, I am pleased to recognize Thorndike Press★ as one of the leading publishers in the large print field.

Founded in 1954 in San Francisco to prepare large print textbooks for partially seeing children, NAVH became the pioneer and standard setting agency in the preparation of large type.

Today, those publishers who meet our standards carry the prestigious "Seal of Approval" indicating high quality large print. We are delighted that Thorndike Press is one of the publishers whose titles meet these standards. We are also pleased to recognize the significant contribution Thorndike Press is making in this important and growing field.

Lorraine H. Marchi, L.H.D.
Founder/CEO
NAVH

★ Thorndike Press encompasses the following imprints: Thorndike, Wheeler, Walker and Large Print Press.

What is impossible with men
is possible with God.
— *Luke* 18:27

Chapter One

"You are not through with men." Dottie Fuller rolled her eyes. The retired high-school drama teacher had worked at the small Santa Barbara antique store for as long as Sierra Summers could remember. With her bright red hair, oversize white-framed glasses and flamboyant clothes, the jovial widow was one of the brightest fixtures in the downtown historic district. "Trust me, you'll go through withdrawal if you cut yourself off cold turkey."

"I'm serious," Sierra said, popping a root-beer barrel from the candy stash behind the counter. Last week's date with her new insurance agent had been fun . . . until she'd discovered he was married. "Men are scum. Brad Pitt could walk through the door and I wouldn't even give him a second glance."

"That's because you don't like blondes," Dottie said with a smile and Sierra had to laugh.

Though she'd only been working with Dottie for two weeks, Sierra had quickly discovered no matter what her mood,

Dottie could always make her smile. "You wait. You think I'm kidding, but I'm not. I —"

Sierra's breath caught in her throat.

Dottie turned from the wall where she'd been straightening a stack of books and followed Sierra's gaze through the picture window at the front of the shop. The older woman's smile widened at the sight of the dark-haired stranger standing on the sidewalk. "Quite a hunk, don't you think?"

"He's okay," Sierra said, with an offhand shrug. But despite her dismissive tone, her gaze remained focused on the man.

He stood talking to a tall blond-haired guy. Sierra dismissed the other man instantly. Jerry's hair had been straw-colored and no matter how much Sierra tried to tell herself that each person was an individual and should be judged on their own merits, guys with blond hair didn't appeal to her.

But the dark-haired man, the one who had first caught her eye, was a different story. Though he had a confident stance usually reserved for men much older, she'd guess he was only in his late twenties. She couldn't tell the color of his eyes at this distance, but his hair was a dark brown, a little too short for her taste, but she had to admit the style accentuated his Grecian profile.

"If I were fifty years younger, I'd go for him." Dottie moved closer to the front of the store and studied the stranger as if he were an actor she was ready to cast in a play. After looking him over carefully, from the bottom of his brown loafers to his khakis to the burgundy chino shirt, Dottie nodded. "He's definitely leading-man material."

Sierra turned and pretended to study a vase shaped like a snake. "He's probably married."

Or a heartless jerk.

"No wedding ring." Dottie shook her head.

"It doesn't matter, anyway," Sierra interrupted the older woman, not wanting to hear the direction of that line of thought. "I told you. I'm done with men."

The German cuckoo clock announced the hour and Sierra shoved all thoughts of the male species aside. It was nearly time to pick up Maddie from preschool.

"By the way, how is the munchkin doing?" Dottie asked. "Has she gotten the hang of that new shoe yet?"

It didn't surprise Sierra that Dottie had followed her train of thought. The woman had an uncanny knack for knowing what she was thinking.

"She's doing better," Sierra said. "And every day she's gaining more strength."

"She's lucky to have you," Dottie said. "If it wasn't for your hard work, she probably wouldn't be walking so well yet."

Sierra just shrugged. Dottie had it all wrong. If she'd been a better mother, Maddie wouldn't have suffered needlessly. She should have ignored that court order and refused to let Jerry take her that day. But even though he was a philandering jerk, she'd never thought he'd hurt his own daughter. . . .

"I'm going to finish cataloguing the new stuff." Sierra headed straight to the back room knowing if she delayed even a second longer, Dottie would notice the tears stinging the backs of her eyes.

Once inside the cool storage area, Sierra took a deep breath to compose herself. She tried not to dwell on the past. After all, it couldn't be changed. But every so often the realization would hit her; he could have killed Maddie.

Thank you, God, for protecting my little girl.

"Pssst." Dottie's voice sounded from the doorway. "There's someone here to see you."

Sierra brushed the remaining tears from her eyes and turned. "Who is it?"

Dottie's eyes sparkled and she giggled. "Guess."

A knot formed in the pit of Sierra's stomach. "Who?"

"Mr. Good-looking himself." Dottie's stage whisper would have reached the back row if she'd been in a theatre. "You know what this means, don't you? You two were destined to meet."

Sierra frowned. "Did he ask for me? Or did he want to see Libby?"

Though on the surface it might seem a strange question, Dottie didn't bat an eye.

"Libby," Dottie said.

Sierra and her best friend Elizabeth "Libby" Carlyle had switched places for the summer. Libby had come up with the crazy idea when she'd decided her money was making her miserable. Still, Sierra hadn't balked. She'd been more than willing to trade in her hand-to-mouth existence for a chance to live the life of a wealthy heiress.

Other than Sierra's mother, Dottie was the only other person who'd been told of the switch. Dottie had labeled the idea "great fun" and had immediately taken Sierra under her wing. Thanks to Dottie's help, the first two weeks of managing Libby's business had gone by without a hitch. But then, no one had ever come asking for Libby before.

"Does he know her?" Sierra asked.

Dottie shook her head. "I don't think so. He asked for Elizabeth."

Sierra breathed a sigh of relief. Only telemarketers called her friend "Elizabeth." "Let me just freshen my makeup and I'll be right out."

"Good idea." Dottie nodded her approval. "Don't rush. I'll keep him entertained and —"

"Excuse me." A deep voice from the doorway interrupted Sierra's thoughts and Dottie's words.

Sierra shifted her gaze and her breath caught in her throat. He was even more striking up close. He stood nearly a head taller than she, and there wasn't an ounce of fat on his lean, conditioned body. And his eyes . . .

Her heart skipped a beat. She'd never seen a man with such beautiful blue eyes. Despite her resolve to keep any and all members of the male species at arm's length, she decided it wouldn't hurt to be friendly.

But though Sierra felt especially cute

today in her low-slung black pants and tiny T-shirt, his gaze remained focused on Dottie. It was as if he'd decided Sierra was just another clerk.

"Mrs. Fuller," he said. "I'm afraid something has come up and I need to go. I'll call or stop back tomorrow."

"But Ms. Carlyle is right —"

"Here's my card," he said, not giving her a chance to finish. "Tell her I'll be in touch."

He gave Dottie a warm smile before shifting his gaze momentarily to Sierra. "Sorry to interrupt."

He was gone before she could respond. Sierra's gaze followed him through the lobby.

"What do you say now?" Dottie's voice held a smug note. "I'd say he's more than just 'okay,' wouldn't you?"

Sierra had to laugh. Though she would have liked to disagree, she wasn't in the mood for one of Dottie's Pinocchio lectures. "You're right," she admitted. "He is a hunk."

"And so familiar." Dottie's eyebrows furrowed in thought. "I know I've seen him before. I just can't place where."

"You've got his card," Sierra reminded her. "Maybe his name will jog your memory."

15

Dottie raised the card to eye level.

"He's probably a salesman," Sierra said. "Or maybe a collector —"

"I can't believe it," Dottie interrupted, her eyes almost as wide as her supersize frames. "I mean, I knew I saw a resemblance. But I never thought . . ."

Sierra rolled her eyes at the older woman's theatrics.

"Give me that." She took the business card from Dottie's hands. "You'd think the guy was famous or something."

Sierra shifted her attention to the card. She read the name. Her smile faded. She blinked and read it again.

A knot formed in the pit of her stomach. "I can't believe it."

Dottie leaned over Sierra's shoulder and stared at the card. She slanted a sideways glance at Sierra. "I told you he looked familiar."

Dottie was right. The resemblance was uncanny. Prickles of alarm skidded up her spine.

Sierra's gaze returned to the card.

To the thick premium card stock.

To the elegant understated lettering.

To the name: Matthew Dixon, Esquire, Attorney-at-Law, Dixon and Associates, Los Angeles.

Dottie's eyes took on a faraway look. "It's uncanny. He's the spitting image of his father at a younger age."

Sierra tilted her head. "Do you know his father?"

"I knew Dix way back when. Before he made it big," Dottie said simply. "But that was a long time ago."

"Was he an arrogant jerk then, too?" A trace of bitterness laced Sierra's tone.

Understanding filled Dottie's gaze and she patted Sierra's hand. "I'd forgotten that I'm not the only one acquainted with him."

"Jerry came out smelling like a rose," Sierra said. "Not only with the divorce but for the child-abuse charges, as well."

It took all of Sierra's self-control to stop there, to stifle the harsh words that would tell Dottie exactly what she thought of Lawrence "Dix" Dixon. The man was a barracuda, a well-known, high-priced L.A. attorney who catered to the wealthy. Messy divorces were his specialty.

The day after Sierra had walked out on her husband, his parents hired Dix to protect their only son's "interests." After all, Jerry was worth millions and California was a community-property state.

The split hadn't been amicable. Though

the divorce petition had cited irreconcilable differences, the real reason could be conveyed in one succinct word: infidelity.

It wasn't as if Jerry could refute her accusations. After all, she'd caught him in the act. Twice.

The first time was when she was pregnant with Maddie. She'd been tempted to leave him then, but Jerry had professed his love, begged her forgiveness and promised he'd never again stray. With their baby's delivery only weeks away, Sierra had more than herself and her feelings to consider. After much prayer, she'd given him another chance.

But a little over two years later, she'd come home early from a neighborhood meeting and discovered his promises meant nothing. This time Sierra had packed her bags, taken her daughter and filed for divorce.

Jerry had gone crazy when he finally realized she wasn't coming back. A couple of times he'd gotten so worked up she'd been afraid he might hit her.

She'd shared her concerns with her attorney and told him she'd didn't want Jerry around Maddie, not when he was so volatile.

But Jerry had no history of violent behavior and Dix had gotten the courts to order that she comply with the temporary visitation order. Against her better judgment, she'd let Maddie go with him that day almost two years ago.

Sitting in that emergency room with her daughter, Sierra had vowed Jerry would never again have the opportunity to hurt her baby. Though Sierra had never planned to take a dime of Jerry's money, she wasn't above using her claim on his fortune as a bargaining chip.

She told him she'd give up all rights to any money if he'd relinquish all parental rights to their daughter. If he didn't, she'd bleed him dry.

To her surprise he'd balked, insisting that he loved Maddie and what had happened was just an "accident." But Sierra had stood firm and in the end Dix had convinced Jerry that accepting the deal was in his best interests.

"Didn't he also handle Stella Carlyle's divorces?" Dottie asked, her words pulling Sierra back from the painful memories.

"All three of them," Sierra said. "Libby always said her mother wouldn't even consider anyone else."

The alarm on Sierra's watch buzzed and she welcomed the interruption. It was three o'clock and her workday was over. Being rich, even if it was just for the summer, held some distinct advantages.

Sierra reached into her pocket and pulled out her car keys, shoving all troubling thoughts aside. She'd promised Maddie they'd go to Dairy Queen for chocolate ice-cream cones after preschool and she wasn't about to disappoint her. "Time to go."

Dottie didn't answer immediately, her mind clearly elsewhere. Two lines of worry furrowed her forehead. "What do you think Matthew Dixon wants with Libby?"

Sierra thought for a moment. Any time an attorney came calling, the news wasn't good. She tapped the card absently against the top of an eighteenth-century gaming table. "I don't know. But after Maddie and I get some ice cream, I'm going to find out."

Chapter Two

On her way to the preschool, Sierra called Libby and updated her on the afternoon's events.

"I don't know why Mr. Dixon's son would be coming around." Libby's voice was thoughtful on the other end of the line. "The only time my mother sees Dix is when she wants a divorce, and since she's not married at the moment . . ."

"Why don't you call him?" Sierra suggested. "Just see what he wants? I've got his number with me. It's 805-682—"

"I'm not calling him," Libby interrupted.

"But shouldn't you at least see what he wants?" As much as Sierra detested attorneys, she realized that with Libby's business interests they could be a necessary evil. "What if it's important?"

"He'll probably stop back tomorrow," Libby said. "Or you can just call him."

"Me?" Sierra's voice came out as a high-pitched squeak.

"Yes, you," Libby said. "We exchanged places this summer so we could get a feel for each other's lives. And, dealing with attorneys is a part of my life."

"But Libby —"

"You're not getting any sympathy from me," Libby said. "Remember I'm the one stuck playing waitress for the summer."

Sierra couldn't help but smile at the long-suffering tone in her friend's voice. "Okay, okay. I'll talk to him."

"Let me know what you find out," Libby added.

"I will," Sierra said. Suddenly a thought occurred to her and renewed hope flowed in her veins. There might be a way out of this yet. "Libby, have you ever met Mr. Dixon? Or his son?"

Sierra crossed her fingers and waited for her friend's answer. If Libby had ever been face-to-face with either man, she was home free.

While Libby had long dark hair and beautiful blue eyes, Sierra's blond hair barely brushed her collar and her eyes were nondescript and ordinary; sometimes looking brown, more often looking green or hazel. The bottom line was, she could no more pass for Libby than Janet Jackson could pass for Madonna.

"Let me think for a minute." Libby paused as if carefully considering the question. "I know I've never met the son. And as far as Dix, I'd have to say no. Stella might not be a candidate for mother-of-the-year but she usually did her best to shield me from her legal battles."

Sierra's smile faded. Now there was no reason she couldn't contact Matthew Dixon. It wasn't that she had anything personal against him, other than his association with the firm. In her mind, Dixon and Associates were the lowest of the low. They catered to the rich. They defended guilty clients. They only cared about winning and the money they'd make off the case, not the truth.

She remembered how hard Mr. Dixon had fought to keep Jerry from serving any jail time on the child-abuse charge. The D.A. hadn't stood a chance. In the end, Jerry had gotten a slap on the wrist: two years probation and four hundred hours of community service.

Maddie had gotten a broken ankle, residual nerve damage in her foot and a lingering fear of men.

Sierra's fingers tightened around the business card. When Mr. Dixon had argued the case before the judge, it was as if the only one who mattered was his client. Poor Jerry who didn't mean to hurt his daughter. Poor Jerry having to answer for what he'd done. Sierra's heart had bled for her ex-husband . . . sharp red drops of hate.

She'd sat in that courtroom and listened to Jerry's lies and excuses and his concerns about his future. It had taken all of Sierra's willpower not to stand up and scream that he'd given up his right to a future when he'd taken out his anger on a defenseless two-year-old.

In the past year, her mother had started encouraging Sierra to forgive Jerry, saying it was the only way she'd be able to truly put the past behind her. Her minister said she needed to forgive as Christ had forgiven her.

Sierra pressed her lips together. Forgiving wasn't an option. Not with the memories of Maddie's sweet little face contorted with pain etched in her soul. Not when Sierra had to watch her daughter struggle to walk again.

It had only been in the last six months that Maddie had been able to run and play like other children. Maybe it was true. Maybe she did need to forgive Jerry to move forward. Maybe she was only hurting herself by holding on to her anger. But right now she hated him for hurting her baby and hated herself even more for not realizing he was capable of such a thing.

"I'll meet with the guy," Sierra said with a resigned sigh.

"I know how you feel about attorneys," Libby said, her tone absolutely serious. "But at least find out what he wants before you let him have it with both barrels. Okay?"

Sierra laughed at the image but didn't make any promises. As far as she was concerned, attorneys were barely a step above the criminals, er clients, they represented.

She'd do her part. She'd listen to what the man had to say. She'd be civil.

But cut him a break? Or give him the benefit of any doubt? Not a chance.

Matthew Dixon took a sip of his iced tea and glanced around the rustic interior of the Chocolate Factory.

It was an unusual place to meet on a bright, sunny afternoon. But he'd made the mistake of letting Elizabeth Carlyle pick the time and location.

When he'd called he could tell she'd hoped to confine their contact to the phone but he'd persisted, offering to meet her any time, any place.

Matt had thought she'd suggest one of

the many State Street eateries where they could sit outside and enjoy the beautiful weather. Instead she'd picked this out-of-the-way restored warehouse. The time she'd chosen was too late for lunch and too early for dinner. It was almost as if she'd deliberately wanted to ruin his day.

He ran his fingers along the inside collar of his starched white dress shirt and tried to stifle his irritation. His father had said that Stella Carlyle wanted her daughter to be personally approached and Matt had complied by setting up this meeting. But even though it was all billable time, money wasn't the issue.

Matt's father had only been working at half speed since suffering a heart attack several months ago and Matt had been forced to pick up the slack. Though he'd been busy with his own clients, it had been nothing compared to the load he had now. His calendar was jam-packed and he had little time to waste. He hoped the woman wouldn't keep him waiting.

Taking another sip of tea, Matt slanted a glance at the watch his parents had given him when he'd graduated from law school three years ago. Ten minutes left. It seemed as though he'd been sitting here forever. But then, he'd arrived early. Traffic on the freeway hadn't been nearly as heavy as he'd anticipated and he'd made good time.

When he'd walked through the front door, the hostess had told him to sit wherever he wanted. Matt had chosen a table that afforded him a good view of the lobby. That way when his appointment arrived, he'd be able to spot her.

Of course, it would help if he knew what she looked like. According to his dad, Stella was an attractive woman; blond and petite. Unfortunately his father didn't recall ever meeting Elizabeth. The only thing he knew about Stella's daughter was that she'd graduated from an Ivy League school, was about his age and owned a small antique store in downtown Santa Barbara called The Hope Chest.

Matt had to smile. Running an antique store was the perfect job for an heiress who wanted to play at being a working woman. He dumped another packet of sugar into his iced tea and decided Elizabeth would probably end up being as flaky as her mother.

"Excuse me?"

A soft feminine voice jerked Matt from his reverie.

"No more iced tea," he said automatically, covering the top of his glass with his hand. "I'm fine."

He kept his gaze focused on the legal brief sitting on the table before him. The waitress had already told him her life story. She'd given him way more information than he wanted to know and Matt wasn't eager to hear any more details.

Silence greeted his words and he briefly wondered if he'd been too curt. Unfortunately, the cute little brunette had made it perfectly clear she was interested in more than taking his order and he didn't want to encourage her. Besides, her constant hovering had begun to grate on his nerves.

"Look, I'm —" He glanced up and the words died in his throat.

The woman standing next to the table was blond, not brunette. She was several inches taller than the waitress and her razor-cut hair brushed her shoulders. Though few women could pull off the trendy disheveled look, the style suited the brown-eyed blonde. The hair framed a face that was a near-perfect oval. Her bone structure was delicately carved but with a hint of underlying strength. The tawny depths of her eyes reflected a keen intelligence and her jaw showed an independence of spirit.

Matt had a vague sense he'd seen her somewhere before.

"Mr. Dixon?" The woman held out her hand. Her voice was husky, low and undeniably alluring. "I'm Elizabeth Carlyle."

Matt pushed back his chair and stood, realizing only now that she was the woman from the storage room. The one he'd casually dismissed as just another clerk, a college student helping out for the summer. It had been an honest mistake, but a stupid one.

If he'd bothered to take a second look, he'd have seen she was closer to his own age than he'd first thought. And she was blond, just like her mother.

He smiled appreciatively, deciding this meeting might not be so bad, after all. "It's a pleasure to meet you, Ms. Carlyle. But, please, call me Matt."

His gaze captured hers. He took her hand and held it, mesmerized by the beauty of her eyes. He was mere inches away from her, and he could see tiny flecks of gold and green mixed in with the mocha-latte brown. Her pupils were surrounded by a tiny ring of gold.

You have beautiful eyes.

Matt wasn't sure if he'd uttered the

words or merely thought them. He only knew he'd never been more sincere. The sounds in the room faded to a distant murmur. They were in a public place but it was as if they were alone, connected by an intangible web of electricity.

Her lips parted and he could see the pulse fluttering in her neck. He had a sudden urge to pull her into his arms, lower his mouth and kiss . . .

"I thought you might like to see a list of today's specials." The waitress materialized out of nowhere, reaching around Elizabeth and slapping the sheet of paper on the table.

Matt gritted his teeth and shot the girl a piercing glance. One that told her he knew exactly what she was up to and didn't like it one bit.

The brunette shrugged and gave him a wide-eyed innocent look. "I'll be back in a minute for your order."

She offered him a sweet-as-sugar smile and walked away, her hips swaying gently.

Matt raked a hand through his hair, heaved an exasperated sigh and turned back to Elizabeth.

She stood staring after the girl, her head tilted.

"Thank goodness she's gone." Matt took

a step forward, a sense of anticipation quickening his pulse. He reached for Elizabeth, fully intending to continue where they'd left off.

But the minute his hand touched her arm, Elizabeth whirled. She jerked back, her eyes bright, patches of pink coloring her cheeks.

Startled, Matt pulled back his arm and let it drop to his side. "Sorry," he said. "I didn't mean to scare you."

The lights from the antique fixtures overhead cast mysterious shadows across her high cheekbones and patrician nose as she looked up at him. Her eyes seemed to glitter, suddenly looking more green than brown or gold. Smile, Matt silently urged. But she didn't. She just stared at him.

He took a deep breath. "I —"

The hostess walked by and gave them a curious look. "Is everything okay?"

Matt nodded, not taking his eyes off Elizabeth. "Everything is just fine."

And everything would be fine, Matt thought, if he could just figure out what was going on. He leaned over and pulled out a chair. "Won't you have a seat?"

She hesitated for only a second, then sidestepped past him, the fragrant scent of her perfume teasing his nostrils and stirring his senses. She moved with the grace of a dancer, looking undeniably fresh and feminine in her silk poppy-print sundress. The leather-and-wood platform slides with hand-painted details complemented the dress perfectly.

Her dress and shoes were the height of fashion. Though Matt wasn't into women's apparel, he recognized a designer's touch. His younger sister Tori had many such outfits in her closet. And from his father's frequent complaints when the credit-card bills rolled in, Matt knew such clothes didn't come cheap.

She wore them well. Matt's gaze lingered admiringly on her long slender legs before he rounded the table and took a seat opposite her.

He leaned back and offered her an easy smile, deciding the best course of action was to simply start over. "I'm glad you could make it."

She lifted her chin a fraction of an inch and regarded him through narrowed amber-colored eyes. "You made it sound on the phone like I didn't have a choice."

He lifted an eyebrow at the subtle challenge in her tone. Sitting there, with that haughty look in her eye, she reminded him of his sister's Siamese cat. Tealock was a nice kitty but she could be difficult, especially when she was riled. He had the feeling the same could be said of Elizabeth Carlyle.

"Even though I realize an attorney can sometimes make an invitation sound like a summons," Matt said with a grin, trying to put her at ease and lighten the moment between them, "I want to assure you that you did have a choice."

Her tense shoulders loosened up and the corner of her mouth curved in a hint of a smile. "You're right," she said. "I could have said no."

"I'm glad you didn't," he said, warming to the topic. "Because if you had, we'd never have met and I'd never have known how beautiful you are."

Her lips tightened and his heart sank. It didn't take a genius to realize it had been the wrong thing to say.

She glanced down at her watch. "I don't have a lot of time so we probably should get down to business. Tell me again what this meeting is all about?"

From the time he'd been fifteen, Matt had enjoyed his share of female attention. And he'd gotten quite good at interpreting their behavior. But Elizabeth was different. She wasn't like most women. One moment she was staring at him with longing, the next she was looking at him as if he'd crawled out from under a rock.

Matt wondered what had made her go from hot to cold in such a short period of time. Did she regret her quick show of emotion? Worry that he'd think she was easy? Could that be why she'd decided to do an about-face and play hard to get?

His analysis was the only thing that made any sense. Satisfied, he settled back in the chair to consider his strategy. Among his fellow attorneys, Matt was considered to be the ultimate competitor. It didn't matter whether it was in the courtroom, on the ball field or in the area of romance, Matt Dixon played to win. Not just *some* time, *every* time.

And this time would be no exception.

Chapter Three

Sierra stared at Matthew Dixon's handsome face and wondered what was wrong with her. She'd never before been tempted to kiss someone she'd just met. But, only a few moments earlier, she'd wanted nothing more than to throw her arms around his neck and kiss him. If the waitress hadn't shown up, she might have done just that and made a big fool of herself.

He was good-looking, she'd give him that. If anything he was even more striking than he'd been that day in the shop. It had to be the suit, she decided. Even a monkey in a silk Armani suit would be appealing.

"Can I get you something to drink?" The waitress reappeared and stood next to the table, pad in hand.

Though the waitress was exceedingly polite, the woman eyed Sierra as if she were a rival, rather than a customer. Sierra smiled sweetly at the girl, wishing there was a way to let her know she was welcome to the man at her table. "I'll have a glass of mango iced tea, please."

"I'll bring it right out." The waitress

turned on her heel and hurried off, leaving Sierra and the attorney alone once again.

Her skin prickled and Sierra could feel Matt Dixon's eyes on hers. The air between them was tense and her heart pounded in her chest. She felt practically lightheaded.

"How do you like owning an antique store?" His lips quirked in a smug smile, and she realized he knew exactly the effect he was having on her.

It was that smile that brought her crashing back to reality.

Arrogant jerk.

Sierra lifted an eyebrow. "Tell me you didn't drive a hundred miles to discuss The Hope Chest."

She'd hoped her coolness would put him off. But if anything, the spark of interest flickered even brighter in his eyes.

"Maybe I did," he said. "How do you know I'm not into antiques?"

Sierra rolled her eyes, finding the teasing tone irritating rather than amusing. "Tell me again the point of this meeting?"

He stared at her, his gaze searching hers. Finally he grabbed his briefcase and set it on the table.

"Your mother has agreed to fund the start-up costs for a private, nonprofit Child

Advocacy Center in Santa Barbara," he said. "She's hired our firm to oversee the project. She'd like you to work with me on it."

The thought was so ridiculous that Sierra burst into laughter. Everyone knew Stella Carlyle's idea of philanthropy was paying her ex-boyfriends to get out of her life. "Mr. Dixon, I don't know where you got your information but my mother isn't interested in civic projects . . . especially ones that involve Santa Barbara."

He lifted his hands in mock surrender. "I'm only telling you what I know."

"You have the wrong woman," she insisted.

He grinned and she noticed he had a dimple in his left cheek. "My father says the planet isn't big enough for more than one Stella Carlyle."

The statement was so on target that Sierra was tempted to return his infectious smile. Instead she shook her head. "It doesn't make sense. She's never expressed an interest in doing anything for this community."

"I don't know how long she's been considering this." He shrugged. "But she specifically told my father she wanted you to be approached about being involved.

37

Though I'm not sure why she just didn't ask you herself."

Sierra's head spun. This was making less and less sense. She couldn't imagine Libby or her mother having an interest in this type of venture. She wanted to ask again if he was positive he had the right Stella Carlyle, but he'd already answered the question once and she doubted his answer would be any different this time.

She folded her hands on the table. "Tell me about these Child Advocacy Centers."

"They coordinate services to children who are victims of abuse." He reached over and took a folder from the briefcase.

Sierra's breath caught in her throat. "Abused children?"

"Both physically and sexually." The light in his eyes dimmed. "It makes me sick. I can't imagine anyone harming an innocent child."

A band tightened around her chest and a lump formed in her throat. Sierra could only nod in agreement.

"A study showed the community has the capacity to provide the services and supposedly there's a need," Matt continued, his voice all business. "Though I have to wonder how much need there is in an affluent city like Santa Barbara."

You'd be surprised to find that child abuse doesn't always happen among the poor, Sierra wanted to say. A familiar ache filled her heart, but she took a steadying breath and forced herself to concentrate on the matter at hand. "Tell me again what my mother's involvement will be?"

"Purely financial," he said. "She'll supply the money. Our firm will oversee the project."

"What about publicity?" Sierra asked, though she was pretty sure she already knew the answer. Both Libby and her mother preferred to stay out of the media limelight.

"The project will be publicized. But your mother doesn't want her name mentioned," Matt said. "At least not until the Center is completed."

"I assume you'll be giving her frequent updates?" Sierra asked.

He leaned forward and rested his elbows on the table. "I'll be giving *you* frequent updates."

A woodsy scent of bergamot mingled with citrus and cloves wafted over her. Sierra inhaled deeply, finding the scent very much to her liking. She shoved the disturbing thought aside, realizing he'd continued to talk.

"Your mother made it very clear that she didn't want to be contacted by our firm until everything is done and the Center is ready to open. I guess she figures she can get whatever pertinent information she needs from you." He paused and tilted his head. "I assume you and she talk frequently?"

Sierra saw no reason to tell him that phone conversations between Stella and her daughter were few and far between. "Do you have any preliminary information about the project?"

He shoved the folder that he'd pulled earlier from his briefcase across the tabletop. "This is what the architects have drawn up so far. I've included articles from other cities where such centers are located as well as some information from the National Children's Alliance."

Curious, Sierra took the packet of information and pulled the papers from the folder. She slowly paged through them, studying each one intently.

"What do you think?" he asked.

She carefully slipped the articles back into the folder. "I just have a few questions. Who is going to have final approval —"

"I'm sorry this took so long." The brunette interrupted, placing a glass of tea in front of Sierra. "Can I get either of you anything else?"

Matt met Sierra's gaze and raised a questioning eyebrow.

Sierra shook her head.

Matt reached into his pocket, pulled out his wallet and handed the girl a twenty. "Keep the change."

The waitress glanced at the bill and a delighted smile blanketed her face. "Wow. Thanks."

He slid the wallet back into his pocket. "Now where were we?"

But Sierra was more interested in the waitress, who was hurrying across the dining room, a new bounce in her step. When the girl disappeared into the kitchen, she shifted her gaze back to Matt. "Why did you do that?"

"Do what?" He raised an eyebrow as if he didn't have a clue what she was talking about.

"You gave her twenty dollars," Sierra pressed. "Twenty dollars for iced tea seems a bit excessive."

Matt shrugged. "She's a real pain in the —" he stopped himself and continued, "but I have to admire her. We were talking before you got here and she told me she takes a full load of classes and works two jobs."

"You made her day." Sierra had worked as a waitress off and on since she was sixteen and she knew how much those unexpected windfalls meant. Because of that, a grudging approval sounded in her voice.

"Waiting tables is hard work," he said, dismissing the compliment. "I'm a big believer that hard work should be rewarded."

Sierra started to tell him that she agreed wholeheartedly. Ever since her divorce she'd been working extra hard to make a new life for herself and her daughter. And she truly believed, with God's help, that one day the hard work would pay off.

But thankfully she came to her senses just in time. She and this man weren't friends chatting about life, they were strangers with little in common. And it was best if they kept anything personal out of their business discussion. "Who did you say has the final approval of the design?"

"You would."

Sierra thought about what the Center would mean to the community. "It's a big project. And it's important it be done right."

"I agree," Matt said. "I'll continue to work with local leaders and the Regional

Advocacy office to make sure the Center meets national standards. You and your mother don't have a thing to worry about."

The underlying assumption was that she should just trust him. While she had to admit that Dixon and Associates was a big-time L.A. law firm, handling celebrity divorces and high-profile criminal cases was one thing, setting up and overseeing a new corporation was another.

"I do have one concern. You're a *divorce* attorney." Her inflection made it clear exactly what she thought of his occupation. "What makes you think you can handle this type of project?"

He stiffened at her disparaging tone and his easy smile tightened. But, when he spoke, his tone was even. "We're a large firm and divorces are only a part of what we do. I can assure you I'm more than capable of setting up a new corporation."

Sierra tapped her fingers against the tabletop. He oozed confidence, but she wasn't convinced. Still, she knew what it would have meant to have such a place when Maddie had been injured. "I don't want this botched up."

"I won't botch it up." Matt spoke slowly, emphasizing each word. His flashing blue eyes let her know he didn't appreciate the insinuation.

It was clear he'd assumed their meeting would be a mere formality. He probably thought this would be the last he'd see of her until the ribbon-cutting ceremony.

But this project was too important to trust to someone like him. Tonight, Sierra would sit Libby down and make her see that they had to be involved.

Libby had to understand this was one venture that simply couldn't be left to an attorney.

Libby Carlyle leaned back in the rattan chair on her veranda and stared at her friend. "You're joking."

Sierra shook her head. "Nope, it's true. Your mother is funding a new Child Advocacy Center."

"Are you sure we're talking about the same Stella Carlyle?" Libby's blue eyes narrowed suspiciously. "We both know my mother doesn't have a philanthropic bone in her body, unless you count the money she donates to Prada."

Sierra smiled. Imelda Marcos had nothing on Stella Carlyle. "Matt seemed confident but I think you should call and check with her, anyway."

"Matt?" Libby placed her cup of Chai on the table and curiosity flared in her brilliant blue eyes.

Sierra stilled. Though she'd refused to call him anything but Mr. Dixon to his face, his first name had slipped past her lips with ease, as if they were best friends and she'd been saying it for years.

She kept her face expressionless. She knew Libby was ready to misunderstand any comments she might make so Sierra chose her words carefully. "Like I said, he had no doubts it was your mother. But I'm certainly not one to trust anything that comes out of a lawyer's mouth."

Thankfully, Libby accepted the statement at face value. She nodded and picked up the cordless phone. "It's got to be a mistake."

Though Libby was acting nonchalant, Sierra could tell by the way her friend's eyebrows furrowed as she punched in her mother's number, that Libby was as puzzled as she was by this strange turn of events. They both knew Stella was selfish and not particularly fond of children. Why she would fund a *children's* center was a complete mystery.

"It's ringing," Libby said, covering the receiver briefly with her hand.

"I'll get us some vanilla wafers." Sierra rose and headed for the screen door leading into the house.

Libby just nodded absently, her ear pressed against the phone.

Sierra had practically grown up in Libby's large Victorian home and the kitchen was as familiar to her as her own. She quickly found the cookies and poured them into a bowl she took from the cupboard. Leaning back against the counter, she ate one slowly. Then, she ate another, nibbling at the edges, prolonging the experience until that cookie, too, was gone.

But the moment Sierra opened the screen door and stepped onto the veranda, Libby's raised voice told Sierra she should have lingered longer. Unfortunately to go back inside would be way too obvious, so Sierra slipped quietly into the chair and averted her gaze to the beautifully landscaped yard.

"Of course I realize that why you do something is your business." Libby's voice was tight and controlled. "It just didn't sound like you and I wanted to make sure —"

Libby paused and even from where she sat Sierra could hear the strident tones in the voice on the other end of the line.

46

"Mother, I'm sorry. I need to go." Libby clicked off the phone and blew out a harsh breath, her face tight with frustration. "What is the matter with that woman? We haven't talked in over a month and yet when I call and ask a few simple questions, she bites my head off."

"Maybe she and Jean-Claude are fighting again." Sierra reached across the table and gave her friend's hand a sympathetic squeeze. She hated it when Stella took her boyfriend frustrations out on her daughter. "You know how cranky she gets when that happens."

"I don't care what her reason is." Libby's eyes flashed. "She doesn't need to be nasty."

"What did she say about the project?" Sierra asked.

"She said she's doing it," Libby said. "She's putting up the money."

Sierra widened her gaze in surprise. Though Matt had been sure he had the right Stella, Sierra had been equally sure it was a mistake. "No way."

"Way," Libby said. "But when I asked why, she went ballistic. Said it was none of my business."

Sierra raised an eyebrow. "Why would she say something like that?"

"None of my business?" Libby's voice rose and she continued as if Sierra hadn't even spoken. "If it's not my business, then whose is it? And why is she being so secretive?"

Sierra lifted one shoulder in a slight shrug. She shared Libby's confusion. Secretive had never been Stella's style.

They sat in silence for several minutes, sipping tea and munching cookies, each lost in their own thoughts.

"The only thing I can figure," Libby said finally, "is that maybe she's getting some great tax write-off."

"And maybe she doesn't want to admit it, thinking it makes her look bad," Sierra added.

Libby nodded. "It's logical. Otherwise the decision to donate seems to come from left field." She paused for a second. "And, before I forget, the attorney was right."

"About what?" Sierra took a small bite of vanilla wafer.

"She doesn't want any updates." Libby lifted her cup of Chai but didn't bring it to her lips. "Says she trusts me to make all the decisions regarding the project. Which is interesting considering she doesn't trust me enough to tell me the reason behind the donation."

"You're going to do it, aren't you?" Sierra leaned forward. "You've got to make sure this project is successful."

"Are you crazy?" Libby laughed as if the thought was ridiculous. "I have my hands full working at the Waterfront and helping your mother with her catering. Besides you have to remember I'm not me this summer."

Suddenly Libby tilted her head and stared at Sierra. An uneasy feeling coursed through Sierra at the look in Libby's eye.

"You'll oversee the project," Libby said, her lips turning up in a satisfied smile.

"Me?" Sierra's heart picked up speed and her hand rose to her throat. "You're the one with the business background."

"You don't need an MBA to give input," Libby said with a dismissive flutter of her fingers. "You've had firsthand experience. You've gone through the process. This will be your chance to give some good input."

"But —"

"Sierra." The look in Libby's eyes said she understood Sierra's hesitation, but her voice was surprisingly hard and unyielding. "Remember when Maddie had to be examined and questioned? You were so frustrated with the system. There were a lot of things you wished could have been done differently, little things that would have made it easier on Maddie and on you. Now, for whatever reason, you have the opportunity to make a difference."

Sierra carefully considered Libby's words. The crazy switch had seemed like such a game but maybe it was all part of God's plan. Maybe He'd put her in this position for a reason. Maybe it was so she could make a difference. There was only one drawback.

"I'll have to work closely with Matt Dixon," Sierra said finally.

"I've seen Dix on television and for an old guy he's pretty hot." Libby's lips turned up in a teasing smile. "If this Matt looks as much like his father as you say, working closely shouldn't be much of a hardship."

"You know how I feel about lawyers," Sierra protested.

"What's that old saying?" Libby lifted a perfectly arched eyebrow. "We all have our cross to bear?"

Sierra sighed. It was clear she wasn't going to get any sympathy from Libby. And though Libby was partially teasing, what she'd said was true. Spending time with an attorney was a small price to pay for the opportunity to make changes that could affect children for years to come.

Yes, Matthew Dixon would be her cross to bear.

But only for the summer.

And only until the project was complete.

Chapter Four

Sierra leisurely swung Libby's BMW Roadster into the secured parking lot down the street from The Hope Chest. It was nearly eleven — almost time for lunch. Though her workday was just beginning, Sierra didn't feel bad coming in at such a late hour.

Dottie managed the early-morning shoppers with ease. After all, she'd been handling them alone ever since Libby had bought the store several years ago. Morning hours weren't Libby's favorite and she'd rarely made it to the shop before noon.

The thought of her friend now having to be at work by eight brought a smile to Sierra's lips. Libby had thought it would be "fun" to be poor for the summer but she was quickly discovering there was nothing even remotely enjoyable about rising at the crack of dawn and working two jobs to make ends meet.

While the switch in positions had condemned Libby to a summer of hard labor, Sierra had been sentenced to one of leisure and she was determined to savor every moment.

There was no "early to bed and early to rise" for her and Maddie this summer. Instead of rushing around in the morning hurriedly downing cold cereal and juice from a box, Sierra cooked waffles, pancakes or eggs and bacon. She hand squeezed Maddie's orange juice and enjoyed coffee made from fresh-ground beans.

After eating, they'd dress and head for the park to play on the swings until it was time for Maddie to go to preschool. Then while Maddie socialized with her friends, Sierra would work for three or four hours before heading back to the Wee Kids Preschool and Child Care Center.

Last week, Sierra had skipped work one day and she and Libby had gone on a shopping spree. Libby had insisted if Sierra was going to play the part of a rich young woman, she had to look the part.

Her frayed jeans and discount-store cotton tops had been replaced by trendy casual clothes purchased from stores without price tags. And playing the part didn't stop with the clothes. Though Sierra had insisted on keeping her apartment *and* her daughter, she'd willingly given up her late-eighties Olds for Libby's new sports car.

Sierra opened the shiny red door and stepped out onto the asphalt, giving the car an appreciative pat. The sky overhead was a brilliant blue and only a hint of a breeze ruffled her hair.

She shut and locked the car but didn't immediately start toward the store. Instead she stood and stretched, inhaling deeply.

It was hard to remember the last time she'd felt so content. Thanks to Libby's scheme, this summer promised to be the best one ever. And the fall was looking just as good. Only one more quarter of classes and she'd graduate. With a college degree she'd be able to snag a good job and that would hopefully translate into a little house, one with a backyard where Maddie and her friends could play.

A fleeting image of the large home on Las Palmas that she and Jerry had shared flashed through her mind. When she'd married her college sweetheart at the end of her junior year, everyone told her she'd hit the jackpot. After all, she was the daughter of a housekeeper while his father was a wealthy land developer. But that wasn't why Sierra had married him. She'd been head-over-heels in love and convinced their marriage would last forever.

The memories of their ill-fated union

threatened to steal her good mood, but Sierra shook them from her head. Jerry was in the past. She hadn't kept his name or his money or his house. She hadn't wanted any of it. All she'd wanted was Maddie.

Sierra headed toward the sidewalk, her smile returning as she remembered her daughter's excited chatter this morning. It was her teacher's birthday and the preschool staff had organized a party. The children had all made cards and they were going to have cake and ice cream for snack. Maddie had been so eager to get through the doors she'd almost forgotten to wave goodbye.

My little girl is growing up.

At one time Sierra had wanted a whole houseful of children, but that was before her marriage had started to fall apart, before she knew what Jerry was really like, before . . .

Sierra blew out a harsh breath and pushed open the door to The Hope Chest. A melodious tinkle of bells announced her arrival. She scanned the eclectic interior, seeing only vases, furniture and baubles. "Dottie?"

"We're here." The older woman's voice sang out from the back of the building.

A brief smile tipped Sierra's lips as she

made her way through the crowded aisles. A small round ice-cream table, circa 1920, sat at the back of the store and she and Dottie often migrated there for a cup of tea and conversation when business was slow.

A deep voice murmured something and Dottie laughed.

The masculine tone came as no surprise. The minute Dottie had indicated she wasn't alone, Sierra had immediately known who was keeping her employee company. Mr. Harlow, from the convenience store two doors down, frequently stopped by on his break. Though Dottie insisted they were just friends, the look in the elderly gentleman's eyes told Sierra that John Harlow was clearly smitten with the vivacious redhead.

Though Sierra sometimes got tired of him being underfoot, she knew Dottie enjoyed the attention. Rounding an Edwardian oak bookcase, Sierra lifted her lips in a welcoming smile.

She stopped short and her breath caught in her throat. An involuntary shiver raced up her spine.

"I see you finally decided to come to work." Matt rose to his feet, amusement lacing his deep voice. A corner of his mouth twitched with a hint of a smile.

It was obvious he was only teasing, but the words still stung. Sierra had been a hard worker all her life and taking it easy didn't come naturally. Sierra could feel her face warm. She started to explain her actions and to justify her late arrival. But at the last minute she shut her mouth and reminded herself that she was the boss for the summer and she didn't need to answer to anyone.

Sierra drew herself up straight and met his gaze with a disdainful haughtiness she didn't even know she possessed. "What can I do for you, Mr. Dixon?"

Though she caught a flash of surprise in Dottie's eyes at her brisk tone, Sierra only lifted her chin higher.

Matt chuckled and grinned. "Did someone get up on the wrong side of the bed this morning?"

He looked so boyishly handsome that she had to smile back.

"Actually, I've been up for hours," Sierra said. Why it was important for him to know she wasn't lazy, she wasn't sure. Maybe it had something to do with the grudging admiration she'd seen in his eyes yesterday when he'd talked about the waitress working two jobs.

"Mr. Dixon brought you something,"

Dottie said, smiling warmly at the younger man.

"Matt," he reminded Dottie, a dimple flashing in his cheek.

"Matt," Dottie concurred and something that sounded suspiciously like a giggle slipped past her lips.

Sierra resisted the urge to roll her eyes at the shameless flirting.

Still, she could see how the older woman could be captivated. After all, the guy had only looked at her yesterday and she'd practically melted. If the waitress hadn't stopped by when she did, Sierra might have kissed him.

There was just something about the man. . . .

He'd risen when she'd walked up and he still stood next to the table. She glanced over to find him watching her. He radiated a vitality that drew her like a magnet and she found herself extremely conscious of his virile appeal.

Sierra tried to throttle the dizzying current racing through her. She met Matt's gaze and lifted an eyebrow. "You have something for me?"

He smiled and held out a manila envelope. "I was on my way to meet with some accountants about the Center and I thought I'd drop this additional information off on my way."

Sierra took the envelope from his hands, her fingers brushing against his, causing her skin to tingle.

Her breath caught in her throat and she looked up to find him staring with a steady gaze.

"You're meeting with the accountants?" Sierra masked her inner turmoil with a deceptive calmness.

He nodded. "Just ironing out some last-minute financials."

"Why wasn't I invited?" Sierra asked.

Matt seemed surprised by the question.

"I didn't think you'd be interested," he said with a shrug. "We're not going to be discussing anything earth-shattering. It'll just be some boring, financial stuff."

Normally boring, financial stuff wasn't something Sierra sought out. In fact when it did cross her path, she usually backed up and ran the other way. But this particular boring, financial stuff related to the Center so she figured she should be interested. And she'd promised Libby she'd be involved.

"I'd like to hear what they have to say," Sierra said. "How about if I tag along?"

The beginning of a smile tipped the corners of Matt's lips. "I'd love to have you come with me."

The door jingled and Dottie rose to her feet with a regretful sigh. "Duty calls."

The older woman cast one last regretful glance at Matt and Sierra before heading toward the front of the shop. There was nothing Dottie liked more than a good drama and this interchange had all the key components.

Sierra swallowed hard, pleased that when she spoke her voice was steady. "What time are you meeting them?"

"Eleven-thirty," he said. "At Crane River."

Sierra recognized the name. The restaurant was popular and well-known for its seafood. Even if the topic was boring, the food should be good. There was only one detail she had to cover. "Who all is going to be there?"

"Dick Johanns, Roger Kirk and myself," Matt said. Pausing, he gazed at her speculatively. "Is there some problem?"

"No problem." Sierra didn't know either of the men so she decided she'd be safe attending. "One more shouldn't make a difference on the lunch reservation, right?"

"There's always room for you," Matt said with a smile. He reached down and picked up his briefcase. "We can ride together if you like. My car is —"

Sierra held up a hand. "It'd be better if we drove separately."

She had to pick up Maddie from preschool at three and though she couldn't imagine the meeting running that long, she didn't want to take the chance.

"Do you know where the restaurant is located?" he asked.

"Actually, Carl, er, a friend and I just met there for lunch last week," Sierra said.

He raised an eyebrow but didn't ask and Sierra saw no reason to mention that Carl Stieve was her church's "family" minister and that he'd spent the entire lunch hour trying to convince her to spearhead First Christian's new outreach program to singles.

Matt's gaze dropped to his watch. "We'd better get going. We don't want to be late."

Sierra glanced down at her sleeveless silk georgette dress with its scoop neck. The color was a golden honey that normally made her look washed-out. But when Libby had seen it, she'd made Sierra try it on then pronounced it "absolutely stunning." The outfit might be a bit too casual for a Los Angeles boardroom, but this was

Santa Barbara and everything was more re-laxed.

"I'm ready," she said. "Unless you think I'll be underdressed?"

His gaze shifted from the mother-of-pearl and semiprecious-stone necklace that circled her neck to the formfitting bodice that hugged her ample curves.

"You're perfect," he said. "I wouldn't change a thing."

Chapter Five

Matt leaned back in his chair and studied Elizabeth over the rim of his coffee cup. The meeting hadn't been half as boring with her by his side.

And not only was she pretty, there was a sharp mind in her blond head. She'd listened attentively and asked appropriate questions, even a few he hadn't considered.

Yes, it had been a good meeting and an excellent lunch, but he hadn't been sorry to see the other men go. Especially Roger. Matt had the feeling if he hadn't been there, Roger would have hit on Elizabeth.

"What did you think of Roger?" Matt asked.

Elizabeth wrinkled her cute little nose, started to say something, then paused. "He mentioned you'd once golfed together. Is he a friend?"

Matt shook his head. "It was some fund-raiser and we got paired together. That was the first and last time I'd seen him, until today."

Elizabeth took a sip of tea. "I'm sure he's a nice man but . . ."

"But?" Matt raised an eyebrow.

"He reminded me of a used-car salesman," she said in an absent tone, stirring some sugar into her tea, "with all that greased-back hair and whiter-than-white smile."

Matt burst out laughing. "I never thought about it before, but you're right."

Startled by the laughter, Elizabeth looked up. He expected her to elaborate but instead her face colored.

"Please forget what I just said. Talking before I think is a weakness of mine." Her voice was filled with embarrassment. "Roger is a perfectly nice man."

"A nice man who is interested in you," Matt said dryly. "The guy had more than business on his mind."

Elizabeth laughed and rolled her eyes. "Yeah, right."

"He did," Matt said. "That's why I put my hand on the back of your chair. I wanted to let him know you weren't available."

Elizabeth's laughter stilled in her throat. "Are you telling me you did that to warn him off?"

Unease coursed through Matt at the look in her eye. He shrugged and forced a nonchalant air. "He's not your type. I was just trying to be helpful."

"I can fend for myself." Her voice was cool. "Besides what if I'd liked him?"

"You don't like him," Matt said. "You like me."

Her eyes widened and her mouth opened but no words came out. He could tell he'd surprised her. Heck, he'd surprised himself.

But the attraction between him and Elizabeth was so strong it was almost palpable. Electricity sizzled between them, feeding off every look, every touch.

"You seem like a nice guy," she said finally. "But —"

"I am a nice guy," Matt said affably. "And, like Roger, I have white teeth. But, that's where the similarity ends."

His efforts to lighten the tension were rewarded with a smile. "On the other hand —"

"Sierra." A tall man stopped at the tableside, his face lighting up. "What a surprise. What are you doing here?"

Sierra?

Matt's gaze shifted to Elizabeth's face. Two spots of pink slashed her cheeks but a pleasant smile graced her lips.

"I was here for a meeting," she answered, not making any attempt to elaborate. "Matt and I stayed after to talk."

The guy stared at Elizabeth for a moment and Matt took the opportunity to study him. He was tall, close to six feet four, with light brown hair, cut short and thinning on top. He couldn't be much over thirty, but his silver-rimmed eyeglasses made him appear older. The conservatively cut three-piece navy suit didn't do much to alter that impression.

Since Elizabeth didn't seem inclined to perform introductions, Matt decided to take the lead. But before he could act the man turned to Matt and stuck out his hand.

"Carl Stieve," he said, giving Matt the once-over. "I'm the Assistant Pastor at First Christian."

Matt pushed back his chair and rose, taking Carl's hand and giving it a firm shake. "Matt Dixon, Sierra's friend."

The name felt somehow right on his tongue. Maybe because he'd never felt that Elizabeth suited her. It had a staid and stuffy sound while Sierra brought to mind a clear mountain breeze. It was a free-spirited name, well-suited to her personality.

The pastor paused, as if waiting for him to elaborate but when he didn't the man just smiled. "Maybe I'll see you in church some time."

Matt offered a noncommittal smile. "Anything is possible."

They talked for a few minutes longer and Matt waited until the entrance door had shut behind Carl, to speak.

He lifted an eyebrow. "Sierra?"

She waved a dismissive hand. "It's a nickname. One from childhood. Most of my friends still call me that."

He looked at her for several heartbeats. "And what should I call you?"

She met his gaze and that now familiar touch of pink dusted her cheeks. "Sierra. But in business dealings, I prefer you call me Elizabeth."

Matt thought for a moment, then nodded. "Makes sense."

"I'm glad you think so," she said wryly. She lifted a glass of tea to her lips.

Matt smiled and sat back in his chair. "Do you and the minister have something going on?"

Sierra choked on her tea, bringing a napkin immediately to her lips. Finally when she seemed able to breathe again, she lifted her gaze to his. "Whatever makes you ask something like that?"

"He looked at you as if you were a ten-ounce sirloin and he hadn't eaten in days," Matt said.

Sierra burst out laughing. "Carl's a vegetarian. And he likes me as a friend, a parishioner, nothing more."

Something about what she was saying didn't ring true. Matt had seen how Carl looked at her and there had been pure masculine interest in the minister's gaze. "Is he married?"

Sierra paused, "No, he's not married."

"Engaged?"

Sierra shook her head.

"Dating anyone special?"

Sierra straightened in her chair. "Carl is too busy to date."

Matt took a sip of coffee. "I bet he'd make time for you."

The challenge hung in the air between them. When he saw the anger in her eyes Matt realized too late that he'd pushed too hard, too fast.

"I don't see how that's any of your business." Sierra's eyes were as cold as jade.

Matt reached across the table and took her hand, refusing to let go even when she tried to pull away. This time, when he spoke he made a conscious effort to keep his emotions under control.

"It is," Matt said softly, "if I'm going

to be your boyfriend."

"My boyfriend?" Sierra stared at him, slack jawed.

"That's right," Matt said, stroking the top of her hand with his thumb. "You can't blame a guy for wanting to know his competition."

"You're not my boyfriend and he's not your competition." Sierra's voice crept up half an octave and she jerked her hand from his. "Why can't anyone understand that I don't want or need a man in my life? I have my family, my friends and my work. That's enough for me. Why is that so difficult to understand?"

Matt considered her for a second. Though on the surface, her words made sense, the strain in her voice told him there was something more behind her vehement declarations. He'd cross-examined enough people to know that what is said isn't usually half as important as what is left unsaid.

"Pastor Carl is putting pressure on you. He wants to be the man in your life."

Sierra started to protest then sighed. "Carl means well."

"But he won't accept the fact that you're not interested," he said softly.

Sierra lowered her gaze but not before Matt saw the look in her eyes. Satisfaction surged as he realized his guess had been right on target.

"It makes things kind of awkward." She lifted one shoulder in a slight shrug and she kept her voice soft and low. "I volunteer a lot at the church so it's not that easy to avoid him. I've tried everything to change his mind, but nothing works. I think he believes that if he persists, he'll win me over."

She raked a hand through her hair and he could hear the frustration in her voice.

Anger filled Matt at the audacity of the guy. If he thought she'd let him, he'd talk to the minister tonight and set him straight. But she didn't seem the type to let someone else fight her battles and he knew he'd have to come up with a more creative solution than confrontation.

"I've got an idea," he said. "When he mentions running into us, just mention we're dating. That should put him off."

"Didn't you hear a word I said?" Her eyes flashed. "I don't want a boyfriend."

"Then we're even." He smiled. "Because I don't want a girlfriend."

She stared, clearly nonplussed. "You don't?"

He shook his head. "Nope."

She hesitated, blinking with bafflement.

"I don't understand."

"If you tell Carl we're dating, he'll back off," he said. "And if you don't want to lie, I'd be willing to take you out a couple of times."

Sierra's mouth twisted in a wry smile. "How benevolent of you."

He grinned. "It wouldn't be a sacrifice. At least not much of one."

Matt leaned forward and cupped her face in his hand. Then without thinking about the wisdom of what he was about to do, he kissed her.

He'd intended it to be a brief kiss, one that would seal the agreement. But the minute his lips met hers, brief wasn't enough. He could feel her arms steal around his neck, her fingers sliding through his hair.

The air stirred around them. He'd been so busy lately he hadn't thought much about women. But as he tasted the sweetness of her lips, he realized that while he hadn't missed the hassles of being in a relationship, he had missed *this*.

"Mommy." A little girl's insistent voice resounded in the quiet restaurant. "I have to go to the baffroom."

Matt ignored the high-pitched whine, but Sierra jerked back and glanced around, her eyes wide and searching.

Matt tugged her back to him. "It's the family in the corner booth. Doesn't have a thing to do with us."

He wanted desperately to kiss her again but she pulled back. It was all Matt could do not to shoot the kid a censuring glance.

"I can't believe I kissed you," Sierra murmured almost to herself.

"It's okay," he teased, trying to lighten the moment. "After all I *am* your boyfriend."

"You are not my boyfriend," Sierra retorted. "In fact, I barely know you."

"There's a strong attraction between us," he said. She opened her mouth to speak but he touched two fingers to her lips. "Don't even try to deny it."

"I admit it," she said with a sigh. "On a superficial level I am attracted to you."

He smiled and chucked her under her chin. "Don't look so glum. That's a good thing."

Sierra looked at him as if he'd gone crazy. She blew an exasperated breath. "It's horrible."

"No, it's not." He spoke with absolute certainty. "There's no way that something that feels so good could be bad."

"Trust me. Lots of things that feel good

can be bad." Sierra's gaze took on a far-away look.

"What was his name?" Matt asked quietly.

Sierra blinked. "Who?"

"The man who hurt you," he said.

Momentary surprise filled her gaze until her lids slipped down over her eyes, hiding her emotions from his view. "It doesn't matter. What matters is that relationship taught me a valuable lesson. I'm better off alone."

"What about certain other needs?"

The pink deepened in her cheeks. The rapid influx of color fascinated him. He'd never known a woman who blushed so easily.

"I keep busy," she said. "Anyway, I don't see where my love life, or lack of, is any of your concern."

Matt paused and carefully considered her response. She might look like a thoroughly modern woman but he was beginning to realize that nothing could be further from the truth. And he had the feeling if he didn't handle this just right she'd be out the door.

"We're in the same boat," he said finally in a matter-of-fact tone. "Two busy people not looking for anything permanent. But an arrangement of sorts could benefit us both."

Sierra looked skeptical but he felt encouraged that she hadn't immediately said no.

Still, her gaze was sharp and penetrating. "I didn't think it was a good idea for an attorney to get involved with a client."

The comment didn't faze him. He recognized it as a last-ditch effort to push him away.

"You're right," Matt said matter-of-factly. "But since I work for your mother and not for you, it's not an issue."

She stared at him for a long moment as if trying to decide if she should believe him or not. "Tell me something. Why you?"

"Why me?"

Sierra nodded. "Why should I turn to you?"

Matt spread his fingers and played them against the table, the image of her in another man's arms doing funny things to his insides.

"A," he said, "It's an easy way to get Carl off your back without being mean."

"But it's not right to lie —"

"B," Matt said, ignoring her feeble protest, "Carl has seen you with me, so your story about us dating will be believable."

"You've thought of everything."

"C." Matt offered her a smile. "You miss kissing and other men's kisses might be laden with expectations."

"Not yours?"

Matt had kissed a lot of women over the years and he'd never been anything but honest. "I decided a long time ago that I'm not even going to begin looking for anything serious until I'm at least thirty-five."

When she didn't comment, he continued. "In the meantime, I'm not interested in living the life of a monk. I don't see any problem with just having a good time, assuming of course that both parties go into the relationship with the same expectations."

"Expectations?" Sierra's voice gave nothing away.

"No commitment, nothing serious. And we'd both take steps to make sure there would be no untoward consequences of our relationship."

"Such as?"

"Babies," he said. "Or sexually transmitted diseases."

Contrary to what many supposed, he hadn't been with that many women. But when he was in a relationship, Matt had never failed to take precautions to protect himself and his partner.

The pink in Sierra's cheeks deepened to a dusky red. "I can't believe we're talking about this."

"It's better to get it out in the open right away," Matt said. "So we're both on the same page."

"But we're not on the same page," Sierra said, her voice rising. "I have no intentions of being intimate with you. So, you don't have to worry about babies and diseases."

Matt frowned.

"My idea of appropriate physical behavior between unmarried adults is kissing and hugging," she said. "It doesn't involve anything more."

Matt paused, trying to make sense of what she was really saying. "Is it that you don't want to do it? Or that you don't want to do it with me?"

"I just met you," Sierra said, a touch of exasperation in her voice.

"So your feelings on the subject have to do with how long we've known each other?"

"No," Sierra said in a firm no-nonsense voice. "It has to do with the fact that intimacy belongs in marriage. My faith teaches that and I've always believed God knew what He was doing when he set up those rules.

"No sex outside of marriage for me," she said. "If you're looking for a summer fling, I'm afraid you're going to have to do your flinging with someone else."

Though Matt wasn't used to anyone telling him no, the sight of her clenched jaw brought a smile to his lips. Ever since he'd met Sierra Carlyle he hadn't known whether he was coming or going.

He liked her sharp mind and quick wit. He liked the fact that she'd chosen to devote time to a project that most women her age could have cared less about.

If he just wanted a no-strings relationship he could easily find a woman who would be more than happy to be with him.

But Matt realized he didn't want just any woman, he wanted *this* woman.

And she wanted him. He could see it in her eyes.

They'd play by her ground rules for now.

But a passionate woman like Sierra couldn't hold out forever. It wouldn't be long before she'd reconsider her decision.

And when she did, he'd be right there waiting.

Chapter Six

"And then I kissed him." Sierra sat back in her chair at the sidewalk café, feeling her cheeks warm. She and Libby had just finished eating dinner when she'd made her confession. It had been over twenty-four hours but the incident was still fresh in her mind. "Or maybe he kissed me. I'm not really sure who made the first move."

"Shut up." Libby's eyes widened and she leaned forward, resting her elbows on the table. "You kissed Matt Dixon?"

Sierra nodded, still unable to believe it herself. The crazy thing was she had the feeling if she were faced with the situation again she'd behave in exactly the same manner.

There was something about the guy. Something about the tone of his voice. Something about the way the light smoldered in his gold-flecked eyes. When his gaze had captured hers, she'd felt as if she were drowning in those liquid blue depths.

"I can't believe you kissed him." Libby's voice rose in surprise. "You hate attorneys. You hate his father."

What Libby was saying wasn't anything Sierra hadn't already said to herself. Yesterday when Matt's lips were closing over hers, Sierra had wondered if she'd lost all her common sense. And last night when the memory of the kiss wouldn't let her sleep, the realization of how easily she'd strayed off course had haunted her thoughts.

She found herself tempted to justify her actions, to assure Libby that Matt was different, that he wasn't anything like his father. But she couldn't say the words because she really didn't know him well enough to defend him. He probably *was* like Dix. After all, what was the old adage? Like father, like son?

"I can't believe it, either," Sierra said with a sigh. "I always thought I had more common sense. Or at least more restraint."

"Was he a good kisser?" Libby's eyes were bright with interest.

Sierra had to smile. Trust Libby to focus on the scandalous part of the tale.

"Amazing." Sierra breathed the word. Even after all these hours, she could almost taste the sweetness of his kiss. "Absolutely amazing."

"Are you going to date him?" Excitement sparkled in Libby's eyes and Sierra knew if she did go out that Libby would insist on hearing every detail.

The thought of interacting without a business agenda between them sent a surge of emotion racing up Sierra's spine. She decided it had to be fear, because it certainly couldn't be excitement. "There's another Advocacy Center meeting scheduled —"

"I'm not talking work." Libby snorted in disgust, not giving Sierra a chance to finish. "I'm talking fun."

"I'm going to tell him it was a mistake." Sierra stabbed a piece of lettuce with unnecessary force. "This just can't be a good idea."

"Of course it's a good idea," Libby said promptly nodding her head decisively.

"How can you even say something like that?" Sierra dropped her fork and pushed away her salad plate, a hard lump forming in the pit of her stomach.

"Because it makes perfect sense," Libby said without missing a beat.

"You sound just like Matt." Sierra picked a crouton off the discarded salad and absently popped it into her mouth. "Did I tell you we saw Carl at Crane River? He stopped by our table to say hello. After he left Matt made sure to tell me that his presence in my life would have the additional benefit of solving my Reverend Carl problem."

"Carl Stieve." Libby scrunched up her nose. "Is the good pastor still calling you?"

"Not as much," Sierra said with a sigh. "But yes, he's still calling."

"Yuck," Libby said, pretending to shiver.

"He's not yuck," Sierra protested halfheartedly. "He's nice. And he's very good with Maddie."

The look Libby shot her was one of shocked disbelief. "Don't you dare tell me you're considering getting serious with Cootie Carl."

"Libby." Sierra kept her tone firm but she couldn't stop her lips from twitching. "No one has called him that since fifth grade."

"At least not to his face," Libby said with a smug smile, tossing her head and sending her dark hair cascading down her back.

Sierra rolled her eyes. Carl Stieve was now an assistant pastor at her church. He was a respected member of the community. Cootie Carl was in the past.

But still, she had to acknowledge that remnants of that boy remained. When Sierra looked into his eyes, she knew he still liked her as much as he had when he was fourteen. A rueful smile tipped her lips at the memory of their freshman year in high school and the afternoon they'd stayed after school to work on a science project.

She'd just started to notice boys. But Carl had been off her radar screen. It hadn't been his most attractive time. He'd been tall and gawky and cursed with a bad case of acne. Though Sierra had since learned the importance of the inner man, at that time she'd been a typical teen and looks had been everything.

But Carl had been incredibly bright and when the teacher had assigned them to be lab partners for the semester, not a single groan of protest had passed her lips. For one thing she knew it wouldn't make a difference. Old man Stoddard didn't like to have his decisions challenged.

But that wasn't the only reason Sierra had kept quiet. She'd seen the look of excitement on Carl's face when the teacher had announced the pairings. He'd been so happy that she couldn't bring herself to burst his bubble.

Even at the tender age of fourteen Sierra recognized that life wasn't easy for Carl. He was tall, but too uncoordinated for sports. And his mother insisted he keep his hair short, instead of slightly longer like all the other boys.

But underneath all that unattractive packaging, Carl was a good guy, a kind soul who cared about others. So she'd just smiled and told him as long as he did all the dissecting, they'd get along fine.

And, it had been a great partnership until they'd stayed late one afternoon to work on a special project. They were alone in the lab and had just finished with a frog when Carl had leaned over and planted a wet, slobbery kiss on her mouth. And that wasn't the end of it. Before she could say a word, or even wipe the wetness from her mouth, he'd confessed his undying love.

She'd turned away so he wouldn't see the tears filling her eyes. Though she felt bad for him, she'd felt just as bad for herself. It figured that her very first kiss would come from Cootie Carl.

Over the years, Sierra had been sorely tempted at several all-girl sleepover sessions to tell all, but she'd kept her mouth shut. The kiss and declaration had remained her little secret. And she'd remained cordial to Carl. Though after the incident she'd made a concerted effort to make sure they were never alone again.

"Carl's an okay guy," Sierra said. "I'm just not interested."

"But you *are* interested in Matt Dixon." Libby raised an eyebrow and took a sip of her iced tea.

Sierra sidestepped the question. "I'll admit I'm attracted to the guy. But I can tell you right now, if I were looking for a relationship it certainly wouldn't be with him."

Libby nodded. "I agree. It doesn't sound like he'd be an ideal candidate if you had marriage in mind. On the other hand, he's perfect for a summer romance."

"He's not interested in anything permanent," Sierra said slowly. "But, then, neither am I."

Sierra pondered the possibilities for a moment. If it would be just temporary, it also wouldn't matter that he was his father's son or a lawyer.

"You see," Libby said with a triumphant smile. "It's a match made in heaven. No ties, no commitments, just fun."

Sierra had to chuckle. "I think God is about commitment."

"Not when you're all wrong for each other," Libby said.

Sierra had to concede the point. Still, though the idea was tempting, it didn't seem right. "I've never used anyone like that before."

"You wouldn't be using him," Libby reminded her. "You'd both go into this knowing the score."

"I wouldn't be intimate with him," Sierra said quickly.

Libby waved a dismissive hand. "Of course you wouldn't. And if he starts to pressure you, you get rid of him."

Sierra silently considered her friend's words. "Some people say you shouldn't date someone you wouldn't want to marry."

Libby rolled her eyes and laughed. "I don't know anybody who says that, much less believes it."

Sierra couldn't help but smile. It did sound kind of silly when you said it out loud.

"Besides, you're not really going to date him," Libby said with a teasing grin. "You're just going to kiss him."

"Thanks for saying that," Sierra said. "That sounds so much better."

Libby leaned forward, her blue eyes dark and intense. "You should do it. Have fun this summer. It might be your last chance for a while. It's not like either of you are expecting this to be a serious relationship.

And it may serve another purpose."

Sierra tilted her head. "What is that?"

"Cootie Carl. I'm sure Matt is right." Libby picked up her drink and regarded Sierra through lowered lashes. "Carl will move on and find another woman when he sees you aren't available."

Sierra shook her head at her friend's confident tone. "You should be in sales."

Libby's eyes brightened as if sensing that Sierra was wavering. "You should do it."

Sierra thought for a moment. All her life she'd tried to do the 'right' thing and where had it gotten her? Anyway, like Libby said, what would be so wrong with just having fun? After all, she wasn't really herself this summer, anyway.

"Why not," Sierra said, for once in her life throwing caution to the winds. "I have nothing to lose. Right?"

Chapter Seven

Matt swung his black Mercedes roadster into his sister Tori's driveway and hopped out. His feet had barely hit the front stoop when the door to her peach-colored stucco town house swung open.

"Matt." Tori's welcoming smile faded and she stopped short, eyeing his dark suit and tie. She glanced down at her striped cotton sundress. "I dressed casual for tonight. Do I look okay or do you think I should change?"

Matt smiled. Even though he knew he was prejudiced, he was firmly convinced his sister would look good in a gunnysack. Her silvery-blond hair was cut short, barely brushing her jawline. She wore it straight and tucked back behind her ears. Her complexion was flawless and she utilized her makeup to full advantage, emphasizing her big blue eyes and full, pouty lips.

"You look great." He was struck once again by how much Tori looked like their mother. Or rather, their mother's pictures. Photographs were pretty much all they had. Janice Dixon had left her husband

and children when Matt was ten and Tori was four.

She'd decided that not only didn't she want to be married anymore, she didn't want to be a mother, either. She'd taken a job with a multinational firm based out of Hong Kong. "I thought we'd just eat at one of the sidewalk cafés downtown."

"But you're all dressed up." Tori glanced down at her dress then back at his suit. "Are you sure you don't want to go somewhere a little nicer?"

"I like eating outside and watching the tourists walk by." He took her arm and pushed her toward the shiny black car. "And I'm only wearing a suit because I came directly from the office. You seem to forget that some of us have to work for a living."

Tori rolled her eyes at his teasing. "Don't give me that. You're on the golf course more than you're in a courtroom."

Matt couldn't help but laugh again. Tori had been born when he'd been six and she'd always had a mind of her own. But he'd adored his baby sister from day one and he still did.

Tori stopped short and stared. "Is this your new car?"

"Yep," Matt said. "Just picked it up yesterday."

"It's absolutely adorable," Tori said, admiring the shiny black finish and plush tan leather seats. "Can I borrow it sometime?"

"Get in," Matt said, having learned early on the value of not dignifying ridiculous questions with an answer.

"Maybe some Saturday night you could let me have it for a few hours?" Tori's gaze grew hopeful. "I'll take good care of it. I promise."

"In the car," he repeated firmly, though he knew he'd probably give in to her pleadings one of these days.

Tori tossed her head and slid into the passenger side. He shut the door and rounded the car. In only seconds he was behind the wheel and they were on the freeway headed toward downtown.

"Dad said something about you and John breaking up," Matt said, turning the volume down on the radio. "I was surprised. You two seemed to get along so well."

"We did," Tori said. "But there were some significant problems."

Matt's fingers tightened around the steering wheel. As children it had been him and Tori against the world and he couldn't stop a surge of concern. John had seemed like a nice guy, but Matt knew people weren't always what they seemed. "Such as?"

"Such as he's determined to move back to Connecticut after graduation and I want to stay here." She lifted one shoulder in a slight shrug. "Even if we could have resolved that issue, he didn't want kids. And I definitely couldn't marry a man who didn't want children."

Matt stared at his sister for a long moment. It seemed like only yesterday that she'd been a little girl playing with Barbie dolls and stuffed animals.

"You're twenty-one years old," Matt said. "You shouldn't even be thinking about marriage and children at your age."

Tori rolled her eyes. "Get real. I've been assessing the marriage potential of every guy I date since I was sixteen."

"You do *what?*"

"My friend Katy's mom always used to say you shouldn't date someone you wouldn't want to marry," Tori said. "Because when you date someone you run the risk of falling in love with them. It made sense to me. That's why I never just date for the heck of it. Beginning with the first date I start checking out their values and where they stand on important issues."

"Issues such as where they want to live?"

Matt asked, trying to keep his tone light and not sound too censuring. "And if they want children?"

"Among other things," Tori said. "I also look at their views on women working outside of the home, their religious faith and if they're ready for a committed relationship."

Matt thought about John. He'd really liked the guy. John had been a go-getter with lots of ambition. And best of all, he'd treated Tori like a princess. "Maybe John would have changed his mind about the children issue."

Tori shrugged. "Maybe. But then again, maybe not. I couldn't take that chance."

"He was a fool to let you go," Matt said.

"My mind was made up," Tori said with a wistful smile. "There wasn't any point in dating him any longer."

"Because you didn't want to become attached to someone —"

"I don't want to marry," Tori said, finishing the thought. The flash of pain in her eyes tore at his heartstrings. "It was hard, but that's the way it usually is when you're doing the right thing."

He wondered what Tori would think about the "relationship" he'd proposed to Sierra. Somehow, he had the feeling she wouldn't approve.

So, on the way to the restaurant he kept the conversation focused on Tori, on her summer classes and the latest movies she'd seen until she shifted the conversation around to his new car.

"I love it," Tori said. "But I have to say I'm surprised. I thought you'd get a coupé. You know, one of those four-doors like Dad drives, one you could use for business."

"I can use this for business." Matt grinned, casting an appreciative gaze around the two-seater. "I just have to limit the number of clients that ride in it at any one time."

"You're such a typical guy. You're all stuck in the adolescent phase," Tori said.

Matt groaned. He should have known he'd regret encouraging her to take that psychology course.

"You refuse to grow up," Tori added.

"If growing up means having an old man's car," Matt laughed, "then you're right, I don't want to grow up."

"I'm not just talking about the car." Tori slanted him a sideways glance, her expression suddenly serious. "I'm also talking about your relationships with women."

"I like women," Matt said. "I always have."

"You're twenty-eight years old," Tori said dryly. "You don't even have a steady girlfriend."

"I'm an old man," Matt said, with a wink. "I'm too tired after working all these hours for any romance."

"You're twenty-eight," Tori repeated. "And you're not even dating. Tell me, how do you expect to find a wife if you don't date?"

Matt tried not to take offense, but something in her tone touched a nerve. It was almost as if she were implying that he couldn't *get* a woman.

"I may not be looking for a wife," Matt said, "but I am dating someone."

It wasn't entirely true. After all, he and Sierra hadn't really been on a date. But they'd discussed the option and that had to count for something.

Interest flickered across Tori's face and she turned in her seat. "Is she marriage material?"

Matt groaned. "Tori —"

"Is she?" The determined look in her eye told Matt she wouldn't let up until he'd answered.

"I don't know," he said finally. "And it doesn't really matter. Unlike you, I'm not looking to get married. At least, not until

I'm at least thirty-five."

"Thirty-five?" Tori's voice came out as a high-pitched squeak. "You'll be practically ready for the nursing home."

Matt grinned. He remembered all too well being twenty-one. Anyone past thirty was definitely over the hill. "I'm hoping I'll still have a few good years left."

"Seriously, Matt," Tori said, her blue eyes blazing with strong emotion. "You don't want to be ancient before you have children."

"That's another thing. I don't know for sure that I want children," Matt said honestly.

"Not want children?" Tori looked at him as if he'd just confessed to shopping at a discount store.

"I don't like kids that much," he said. "They're messy and loud and they demand a lot of attention."

Tori's eyes widened and for once she didn't have a comeback, she simply stared in stunned silence.

Matt changed the subject, relieved he didn't have to elaborate. His arguments sounded good and they were true as far as they went, but he had deeper concerns, ones that he didn't feel like sharing, even with his sister.

Though he wasn't keen on kids, one of his big concerns about going the parenthood route was he didn't think he'd be very good at it. From what he'd observed, most successful parents learned their skills from observing their own parents.

The only man Matt had to model himself after was his dad. Though Dix had tried, he'd certainly never win any parent-of-the-year honors. He'd done his best after his wife had left, but he'd had very little interest in parenting his motherless children and had relied on employees to see to their needs.

Matt shoved the disturbing thought aside and pulled into a parking space on the street just around the corner from the Italian restaurant. He stepped out and rounded the car, opening Tori's car. Once the alarm system was activated, they started down the sidewalk.

Santa Barbara was a casual town and Tori fit in perfectly. She wiggled her fingers and smiled at a guy in shorts and a pair of flip-flops walking his dog down the street.

"That's Kyle," Tori said. "He's hot."

"How do you know him?" Matt asked before giving the hostess at the sidewalk podium his name.

Tori smiled. "He's in physics with me."

Matt lifted an eyebrow. "A potential mate?"

"Shut up." Tori punched him in the arm.

"I'm just asking," Matt said with a slight shrug. "After all, you did say he was hot. I would assume physical attraction is part of your assessment criteria."

"I am attracted to him," Tori said with a regretful sigh. "But I'm a Christian. He's an agnostic. It wouldn't be a good combination."

"So he's out?"

Tori nodded and gestured with her thumb. "Out."

Matt shook his head and couldn't help but laugh as they followed the hostess to a table in the sidewalk dining area. "Got any other prospects in mind?"

Tori smiled at the waiter as he pulled out her chair and placed the menu before her. "I'm tired of talking about me. I want to talk about *you*. I especially want to hear about this new woman you're dating."

"There's not much to say." Matt picked up her menu and handed it to her with a pointed glance. "They've got great Fettuccini Alfredo here."

But Tori didn't look at the menu. Instead her gaze had shifted toward the inside of the restaurant.

"I want that woman's belt," Tori said

abruptly. "The lambskin one. I have a friend who has one just like it."

Matt followed the direction of her gaze and his eyes widened. It was Sierra. She wore a multicolor stretch cotton skirt and a white sleeveless top. The belt his sister admired was wrapped around her trim waist.

"Beautiful," he breathed. She'd pulled her hair back from her face with some kind of cloth band that complemented her skirt. Her eyes were large and green and a touch of color brightened her lips.

"Will you buy me that belt for my birthday?" Tori shifted her gaze back to him. "Dad won't do it. He says it's way too expensive."

"Sure," Matt said idly watching Sierra slowly weave her way through the crowded tables and out onto the patio in their direction.

"I knew I could count on you." Tori reached over and squeezed his arm. "Anyway six hundred dollars isn't that much. Not for lambskin."

Matt's gaze briefly jerked to his sister. "How much?"

"Six hundred," Tori said with an innocent look that didn't fool him in the least.

"Forget it." Matt pushed back his chair

and rose to his feet. As if Sierra could feel the heat of his stare, her steps slowed and for the first time she looked in his direction.

"Matt." Surprise filled her voice and she walked over. "Did you just get here? I didn't see you before."

Her gaze flickered briefly over Tori and Matt quickly performed the introductions.

"It's nice to meet you," she said pleasantly, shaking Tori's hand. She nodded to Matt. "Good to see you again."

"I love your belt," Tori said.

Sierra glanced down as if she'd forgotten what she'd put on. "It's lambskin."

"I know," Tori said. "My friend Marlys has one just like it."

Sierra smiled again.

"Sierra." A feminine voice called out.

Sierra turned immediately. A brunette sat at a table on the edge of the outdoor seating, holding up a cell phone.

Sierra nodded before turning back to Tori. "I'm afraid I need to go."

Matt could tell she was in a hurry. Still, he couldn't let her go, not quite yet. He touched her arm and met her gaze. "We need to talk."

Uncertainty flickered for a moment in her eyes before she nodded. "I'll be home after nine."

"I'll call," Matt promised.

She inclined her head in a slight nod, said goodbye and walked away.

"Is there something going on between you two?" Tori asked, her gaze following Sierra to the table.

"She's my new girlfriend," he said.

Tori's eyes widened and her gaze jerked back toward Sierra. "Why didn't you say that when you introduced her?"

Reproach colored Tori's question. Matt ignored it.

"It's a relatively new relationship." He shrugged. "I didn't want you interrogating her. It's enough that I introduced you."

"Does the fact that I've met this one mean she's special?" Tori asked. "Will she be around for a while?"

"I doubt it," Matt answered honestly. "She's not looking for anything long-term, either."

"Don't tell me she's like you." A look of horror crossed Tori's face. "Surely *she* doesn't want to wait until she's in her thirties to settle down."

"I don't know," Matt said with a shrug. He had no idea what Sierra's thoughts were about marriage. But then he couldn't honestly say he knew much about her thoughts on anything. But if he had his way, they'd soon get to know each other better.

His gaze shifted and settled appreciatively on Sierra's curvy figure.

Yes, he'd like to know her much better.

And that couldn't happen soon enough to suit him.

Chapter Eight

Sierra patiently answered her mother's question about the timing of Maddie's allergy medication and then spoke with her daughter briefly before hanging up. She handed the phone back to Libby.

"Is everything okay with Maddie?" Libby asked.

Sierra smiled, remembering how her daughter had chattered happily about her evening with her grandmother. "She's fine. She and my mother are having a great time."

Libby nodded absently, her attention focused on Matt and his sister.

"Who's the handsome hunk you were talking to?" Libby asked.

"You don't recognize him?" Sierra asked in surprise. "Everyone says he's the spitting image of his father."

Libby's gaze returned to the dark-haired young man. "Lawrence Dixon's son?"

Sierra nodded.

"Who's the girl?"

Sierra lifted her glass of tea that the waitress had refilled and took a drink before she answered. "That's his sister, Tori."

"His sister?" Libby shook her head. "Having dinner with a woman you're related to is a complete waste of those good looks."

Libby took a sip of water and studied Matt beneath lowered lashes. "He's so cute. I can't believe he's not involved."

"He's so arrogant, who would want him?" Sierra said.

Libby smiled, her appreciative gaze still lingering on Matt. "You'd be surprised. I can think of a dozen women off the top of my head who'd like him."

Something in her friend's voice made Sierra pause. "Are you saying *you* want him? 'Cuz if you do, you're welcome to him."

Libby laughed out loud. "In case you've forgotten, I have Carson. I can only concentrate on one man at a time."

Sierra wondered how she could have forgotten. After all, Carson Davies was all Libby talked about lately. Only in his late twenties, he already owned a restaurant on the pier. He was also Libby's boss for the summer. With his sun-bleached blond hair and a surfer's body, the guy had captured Libby's attention from the moment she'd walked through the door pretending to be Sierra.

"Besides," Libby added, "Matt is *your* boyfriend."

Sierra thought about arguing the point, but what did it matter?

The "William Tell Overture" filled the air and Libby reached for her cell phone.

Sierra frowned. "It's not my mother, is it?"

Libby glanced down at the phone. "I'm not sure who it is."

"Hello," Libby said, then rolled her eyes, pointed a finger to her chest and mouthed the word "mother."

Sierra sat back in her chair and studied the tourists passing by on the street until Libby hung up.

"That was the weirdest call," Libby said.

Sierra lifted an eyebrow.

"I can't believe it. Mother really *is* interested in the Child Advocacy Center," Libby said. "She called to find out if I'd met with Matt Dixon yet."

Stella Carlyle inched up a notch in Sierra's estimation. It was nice to know the woman wasn't as shallow as she'd always thought.

"Mother seemed truly interested," Libby repeated.

"She wanted to hear every detail of our meeting. For a second I wondered if she trusted the man. But I think she was just curious about everything. She even wanted to know what Matt looked like."

Sierra's eyebrows drew together. "What does it matter what he looks like?"

"It doesn't." Libby lifted one shoulder in a slight shrug. "But then it doesn't really matter what the outside of the Center looks like and she wanted to know all about that, too."

"You let her know that Matt was doing a good job, didn't you?" Sierra didn't know why she asked, other than she knew how important this project was to him.

Libby nodded. "I said he was doing a fabulous job. Didn't you hear me bragging him up?"

"What did Stella say to that?"

"She seemed pleased," Libby said. "Especially when I told him that I thought we worked well together. I even mentioned that I hit it off so well that we've started seeing each other socially."

Sierra frowned in confusion. "Why did you tell her that?"

Libby wrinkled her nose. "It was a spur of the moment thing. Besides, you're me this summer and the two of you *have* started dating."

"Lib-by, Lib-by, Lib-by." Sierra shook

her head. "You shouldn't tease your mother like that."

"I couldn't resist," Libby said with a smile, seeming not the least bit sorry. "She just seemed so interested in everything that I decided to give her what she wanted and —" Libby's smile widened "— maybe a little bit more."

Sierra could see she wasn't getting anywhere with her friend. From the time she'd been little, Libby had loved to "get her mother going" and this time would be no different. Sierra heaved a resigned sigh. "Okay, but will you at least promise me one thing?"

Libby's gaze was questioning.

"Don't embellish it too much, okay?" Sierra asked.

With all the innocence of a seasoned veteran, Libby widened her eyes. "What are you so worried about?"

"That if you keep up this charade, by the time the summer is over, your mother will have you married to the guy," Sierra said.

Laughter crinkled the skin around Libby's blue eyes. "That would never work."

The agreement came too quickly. Sierra narrowed her gaze. "It wouldn't?"

"Of course not," Libby said, a wicked

twinkle in her gaze. "If anyone marries the guy, it'll have to be you."

After dropping off Libby, Sierra headed for her apartment on the town's northern edge. Although her daughter loved to spend the night with her grandmother, Maddie had an early-morning play date with a friend and that meant tonight she'd be sleeping in her own bed.

Her mother and Maddie were so intent on Candy Land they didn't react when Sierra stepped into the living room. Just as Sierra was about to clear her throat, Maddie looked up. Pure joy crossed the little girl's face and she immediately jumped to her feet. "Mommy."

Maddie raced liked an out-of-control train across the living room. Her tiny body hit Sierra with a thud and she wrapped her arms tightly around her mother's legs. "I've missed you so much."

Sierra knew that Maddie had probably been having so much fun with her grandmother that she hadn't had time to give her a second thought. Still, the sweet words made Sierra's heart swell with love. Though she deeply regretted her marriage to Jerry, something good and beautiful had come out of the union.

Her hand stroked her daughter's tousled blond curls and when she spoke her voice was thick with emotion. "I've missed you too, pumpkin. Did you and Gram have fun?"

Maddie took a step back and her blue eyes danced. She nodded her head vigorously. "We had ice cream and cake and —"

The little girl paused and her eyebrows pulled together. She cast her grandmother a beseeching glance.

Peggy Summers smiled, love and pride reflected in her eyes. "Fruit punch?"

" 'N punch." Maddie's smile widened. "It gave me a stash. But Gram said that was okay."

"A rash?" Sierra's heart rose to her throat. Her gaze darted to her mother. With all of Maddie's allergies, didn't her mother realize that an unexpected rash could indicate a serious reaction. "Why didn't you call me?"

Sierra didn't wait for a response. Her hands moved to Maddie's shirt. She couldn't see any red spots on her arms and legs, so it had to be on her chest or back. Though her mother had apparently dismissed it as trivial, Sierra needed to see for herself.

Maddie laughed and brushed aside Sierra's hands as if it were a game, her giggle at odds with the tight coil of tension gripping Sierra's gut.

"Honey, there's nothing to worry about," Peggy said in a reassuring tone. "Maddie had a mustache, not a rash."

Mustache?

For the first time Sierra noticed a faint red color on her daughter's upper lip. She exhaled the breath she'd been holding.

If anything ever happened to Maddie . . .

"She's fine," Peggy said as if she could read her daughter's thoughts. "Aren't you, pumpkin? Tell Mommy you're filled to the brim with ice cream and cake."

Maddie smiled broadly, showing a missing front tooth. " 'N punch."

"Punch, too?" Sierra tried to join in the spirit, but the fear had left her drained.

Maddie nodded happily.

Sierra cast her mother a questioning glance. Though she didn't mind her daughter having a treat now and then, it sounded as if tonight had been a junk-food feast.

Peggy rose to her feet and straightened her skirt.

For the first time Sierra noticed her mother was dressed in the new skirt and blouse she'd bought last weekend.

"Maddie and I went to Frank and Lynn's anniversary party tonight," her mother said in response to Sierra's questioning glance. "They were going to celebrate on the weekend, but their plans changed. Her sister is leaving town earlier than expected so they changed the party to tonight."

Her mother had been Lynn's maid of honor thirty-some years ago and they were still good friends. Guilt sluiced through Sierra. She'd never have asked her mother to baby-sit if she'd known tonight was Lynn's anniversary celebration. "You should have told me —"

Her mother cut her off, casting a pointed glance at Maddie. "Everyone was glad to see Maddie. You would have been so proud of her. She was very well-behaved."

"I said please and thank you," Maddie said. "And I ate my cake with my fork."

The little girl made the announcement with such emphasis that Sierra knew her mother must have coached her and then praised her extravagantly for her efforts.

Thank you, God.

The prayer of thanks was for both of the women in her life. God had truly blessed her. Though her life hadn't been without trials, she'd had her mother's love and support every step of the way. And now her mother was showering the same unending supply of love on Maddie.

"Sounds like you girls had a fun evening," Sierra said, emotion making her voice huskier than normal.

"We did." Peggy moved across the room to stand close to her daughter. "A busy day and a fun evening. But now we're both tuckered out."

It was only eight-thirty. Sierra knew her mother rarely went to bed before midnight, but Maddie's eyes were already drooping.

"I want to play another game." Maddie whined, dropping back to her knees and shoving the Candy Land board aside.

Sierra's gaze met her mother's and they exchanged a knowing look.

"Maddie's already had her bath and brushed her teeth," her mother said in a low tone. "She's exhausted but won't admit it."

Sierra took note of her daughter's petulant expression. It looked like bedtime was going to be a struggle. She heaved a resigned sigh and turned her attention back to her mother. "I'm sorry you had to take her —"

Peggy laid her hand on Sierra's arm.

"Not another word," Peggy ordered in

that same no-nonsense tone she'd used on her when Sierra had been Maddie's age. "I was happy to have her. Some of my friends hadn't seen her in a while and this gave me a chance to show her off."

The pride in her mother's voice warmed Sierra's heart. "She's a good girl."

"Yes, she is," her mother said.

"Can you stay for a cup of coffee?" Sierra asked. "I'd love to hear all about the party."

"I wish I could." A tinge of true regret laced Peggy's tone. "But if I stay, Maddie won't want to go to bed."

"I can't find it." The urgent whine over a missing board piece told Sierra that Maddie was rapidly approaching meltdown.

"You're right." Sierra blew out a disappointed breath. Though she and her mother were close as sisters and talked every day, Sierra hadn't seen her mother as much since the switch. Impulsively she gave her mother a quick hug. "Thanks so much for watching her."

"We had a lovely time," Peggy said, a smile of remembrance lifting her lips. "Reverend Carl was at the party. He asked about you. He's so good with Maddie.

Why he isn't married with children of his own, I don't know."

"Maybe he's just never found the right woman," Sierra said lightly.

She wished she would have kept silent when a speculative gleam filled her mother's eyes. "Maybe he has found the 'One' but she doesn't know it. He talked about you constantly."

Sierra tried to quell her irritation. "I'm surprised. I barely know the man."

The words slipped past her lips before she had a chance to consider their impact on her mother. Peggy had the utmost respect for men of the cloth and in her eyes, Carl was practically perfect.

Her mother's lips pursed together and though she'd said nothing bad about the man, Sierra had a crazy impulse to apologize.

"You went all through school with him," Peggy pointed out when Sierra remained silent. "He's the assistant pastor of the church you attend every week. I think you know him a bit more than barely."

Sierra bit back the desire to tell her mother the truth was, that she already knew him better than she wanted. Instead she lifted a shoulder in a slight shrug. "You're right. I do know Carl. And he is a nice guy. It just makes me uncomfortable to have him talk about me when I'm not there."

"I think he's sweet on you," Peggy said, nodding her head at the conclusion. "I really think he'd like to date you. And you couldn't find a better man."

"I'm already dating someone," Sierra said before her mother had a chance to visualize her and Carl walking down the aisle. And, though "dating" wasn't exactly accurate, "I'm kissing someone," wasn't something she felt like saying to her mother.

"You are?" Her mother's eyes widened in surprise and the look on her face would have been laughable at any other time. "Who?"

"Someone I just met," Sierra said quickly. "His name is Matt and he's involved with the Advocacy Center fundraising."

She didn't mention his father's connection to Jerry. If her mother knew Matt was Dix's son, she'd never believe that Sierra would date him.

"Is this Matt the man Carl saw you with at Crane River?" Her mother tilted her head and her gaze grew sharp and assessing.

"Crane River?" Sierra asked stupidly.

"Carl mentioned he'd run into you and a male friend the other day over lunch," her mother said. "I could see it had shaken him. He wanted the scoop but I had to tell him I didn't know anything about the man. He asked if I thought it could be serious and I told him I'm sure it wasn't, because otherwise I'd have met him."

Sierra could see the hurt in her mother's eyes. At the moment she wasn't sure if it was the not knowing that bothered her mother or the fact that Sierra didn't seem to return Carl's interest.

For years her mother had harbored the hope that she and Carl would get together. She'd told Sierra on more than one occasion that she would make the perfect minister's wife. Though for a split second, Sierra had considered coming clean with her mother, she now rejected the option. It would be best to let her mother think she was interested in Matt.

Otherwise, Sierra could envision the next few months. Her mother would be inviting Carl over for dinner and encouraging Sierra in a million other less obvious ways to give the good pastor a chance.

Sierra knew she'd disappointed her mother when she'd married Jerry. Though at the time everyone had thought Jerry was a great catch, her mother had voiced strong reservations about the union. And time had proved her mother's instincts correct.

But she's not right in this case.

Sierra's hands tightened into fists at her side. Reverend Carl was not the man for her. He couldn't be. No matter what her mother thought.

Actually, after her divorce she'd vowed to swear off men entirely. She didn't need a guy in her life to be happy. She had a daughter to raise and Maddie was her priority.

She'd thought her mother would agree when she'd said as much to her one day. But to her surprise Peggy would hear none of such talk. She wanted Sierra to marry again, to find the true happiness that had eluded her the first time around. And, from the look in her mother's eye, Peggy was convinced Sierra would find that happiness with Reverend Carl.

If she were an impartial bystander, Sierra might agree. On the surface she and Carl had everything in common: background, values, faith. He adored Maddie and would make a wonderful father. Many would argue, a successful marriage between the two was practically guaranteed.

But every impractical part of Sierra's being railed against that conclusion. Carl didn't make her pulse leap when he walked into a room and his long-ago kiss had repulsed rather than excited her.

There's more to life than sexual attraction, she scolded herself. Look at Jerry. Her heart had done flip-flops whenever he was in the room and look how that had ended.

"Sierra?" Her mother's voice jerked her back to the present. "Who is this new man in your life? Why haven't you mentioned him?"

"I hadn't mentioned him before because our relationship —" Sierra's tongue stumbled over the word "— is fairly new."

It wasn't exactly a lie, she told herself. Their business relationship *was* brand-new. When, or if, a personal one would ever get off the ground was anyone's guess.

But, Sierra realized suddenly, it wasn't anyone's guess, it was up to her. Matt had made her an offer and it was up to her to accept it or not.

"You must like him," Peggy said.

Sierra thought for a moment then nodded. "Well enough, anyway."

"Other than Carl and the insurance

agent, he's the first man you've dated since Jerry," Peggy added.

Her mother was right, but instead of it scaring her, the thought gave her a measure of comfort.

A relationship with Matt would be like sticking her toe into the water rather than jumping in feet-first. She could get used to the water, then at the end of the summer when the project was over and Matt was long gone, she could decide if she was interested in getting back into the dating game or not.

Yes, when you thought about it, spending time with Matt this summer made complete sense.

"Matt is nice," Sierra said to her mother. "But neither of us is looking for anything serious. Not at this point, anyway."

"What religion is he?"

The question took Sierra by surprise. The minute she'd mentioned she was dating someone she'd known an interrogation would be forthcoming, but she hadn't expected it would start tonight. Sierra blinked, thought about lying, then decided to be honest. "I'm not sure."

Her mother's gaze narrowed. "Haven't you talked about your faith with him?"

"It hasn't come up," Sierra said,

knowing it wasn't much of an answer. Unfortunately it was the truth.

Her mother pursed her lips. "Does he like children?"

The casual tone and offhand manner didn't fool Sierra. "We haven't talked about children, either. Like I said, the relationship is brand-new."

Sierra wished she could tell her mother not to worry, that Matt was the last man Sierra would ever seriously consider. And it didn't matter what he thought about God or children because he would never meet Maddie, and he would certainly never be a part of their life.

"Maddie." Sierra turned to her daughter, who was rummaging through the toy box. "Help Gram and me pick up the toys."

Maddie whirled, her bottom lip protruding. "I don't want to pick up, I want —"

Sierra straightened and favored the girl with the look she'd perfected the past four years. Though she and Maddie were close and Sierra loved the little girl with all her heart, she was determined to raise a well-adjusted, well-behaved child.

Maddie stared at her mother for a long moment. "Okay," she said finally, only a trace of sulkiness in her tone. "But first I have to give Gram a hug."

The little girl propelled herself across the room and lifted her arms to her grandmother. "I love you, Gram."

Sierra and her mother exchanged a smile. Maddie still hadn't realized that there was no divide-and-conquer when it came to the two women in her life.

"I love you too, pumpkin," Peggy said, sweeping up Maddie in her arms and giving the girl a big bear hug before setting her back down. The older woman's gaze shifted to the Candy Land boxes. "Do you think you can put all the pieces in those little slots all by yourself? Or do you need Gram to help you?"

Maddie shook her head vigorously. "I do it myself."

It was all Sierra could do not to laugh. The response was just what she'd expected from her independent daughter.

Sierra smiled and picked up a stuffed pig with ten Velcro-attached piglets lying on a chair. With a wide arching lob she tossed the pig family into the toy box.

God had blessed her with faith and family. She had everything she needed. Who could ask for anything more?

Chapter Nine

Sierra checked on Maddie one more time before she slipped into the shower. The water's cool spray was invigorating and she hummed as she dried off and slathered lotion on her body. She'd just wrapped a towel around her head and pulled on the silk robe her mother had given her for Christmas when the phone rang.

Praying the loud ring wouldn't wake Maddie, Sierra shot out of the bathroom, sidestepping a headless Barbie in the hall. She reached the living room in record time, her hand clicking the cordless phone on the minute her fingers closed around it. "Hello."

"Hey, beautiful." The deep masculine voice filled the phone line. "What's up?"

"Who is this?" Sierra forced an innocent tone.

Silence filled the line for a second. "It's Matt. Who did you think it was?"

"It could have been any one of my many admirers," Sierra said airily, smiling at the thought of how easily she'd taken the wind from his sails. "That's why I always ask."

"Many admirers, huh?" Matt asked. "Like Reverend Carl?"

Sierra laughed and dropped to the sofa, ignoring his question. "You called at a good time. I just got out of the shower."

A brief pause greeted her words and she didn't have to see Matt to know there was now a wicked gleam in his eyes.

"Sounds exciting. Can I come over?"

Sierra shook her head and her smile widened. Matt might not have all of Carl's virtues, but he was fun.

"Have you heard the saying 'the early bird gets the worm'?" She plumped up an accent pillow and made herself comfortable against the overstuffed cushions. "Well, you're five minutes too late. I have my robe on. And you live too far away, anyway."

"Didn't I tell you?" he asked. "I've moved to Santa Barbara for the summer. If our new office works out well, the move may be permanent."

"No way." Her heart caught in her throat and she wasn't sure if it was dread or excitement coursing through her veins. After all, it was one thing to have a casual relationship with someone who lived out of town, quite another when they could be only blocks away and close enough to call any bluff.

"Don't sound so enthusiastic." His voice was quietly teasing and she could almost see the grin spread across his face.

"It doesn't matter to me where you live," Sierra said, waving a dismissive hand even though he wasn't there to see it.

"Sure it does," he asserted. "Or it should, anyway. After all, you are my girl-friend."

"In name only," she reminded him.

"I beg to differ," he said placidly. "In name only would mean our relationship is purely platonic. Kissing each other changed that."

"It didn't change anything," Sierra said. "In name only means no emotional in-volvement. It means you can kiss someone for no better reason than you feel like it."

"Hmm." A thoughtful air filled the line and she had the feeling that instead of blowing off her words, he was carefully considering them. "Makes sense."

Sierra hadn't expected him to agree. And she wasn't sure why it bothered her to have him concede the point. "I need to go."

"Why?" he asked, clearly startled by her abruptness.

"I'll talk to you tomorrow," she said. "Good night, Matt."

"Wait," he said quickly. "Before you hang up I have something to ask you."

"Make it quick."

"James Hanna, the main architect for the Advocacy Center, is having a party at his house on Friday night. It would be a good idea if we went together."

"Absolutely not," The words popped out of her mouth the same instant they entered her head.

"Tell me what you *really* think." Laughter filled the other end of the line.

While Sierra conceded her response had been a bit rude, it was honest. Not because she didn't like him but because a party typically meant lots of people. Lots of people meant someone could be attending who knew Libby. Someone who knew Sierra wasn't Elizabeth Carlyle.

"Saturday just isn't good for me," she said.

"Even on the phone you're cute when you lie." He laughed again. "The party's on Friday."

"Oh." Sierra paused, sure he'd said Saturday. But she wasn't about to argue. She didn't plan to attend the party whether it was on Friday or Saturday. "I don't think it's a good idea to mix business and pleasure."

"I agree," he said without missing a beat. "This party is strictly business."

"I don't believe you," she said.

"Scout's honor."

She could almost see him holding up three fingers in the Scout salute and she had to shake her head at the depths to which the man would go to get his way.

"Now who's lying to who?" Sierra couldn't resist teasing him. "We both know you were never a Boy Scout."

"I had friends who were Scouts," Matt said. "That should count for something."

"It doesn't count," Sierra said.

"I wanted to join but my father didn't have time to take me to the meetings," Matt said. "Surely that counts."

"It's definitely a stretch," Sierra said, playing along. "What about your mother? Why couldn't she take you?"

"She left when I was ten," he said and for a second Sierra swore his voice hitched. But a chuckle dispelled that notion. "And Dad had better things to do than shuttle me around to campfires."

"It's hard for one parent to do it all," Sierra said softly. That's why, way back when, she'd sworn to herself that *her* children would grow up with both a mom and a dad.

She sighed. "I know. I grew up without a father."

"I remember my dad talking about that divorce," Matt said. "Sounded like it was an ugly one."

For a second, Sierra couldn't figure out what he was talking about. Her father had died in an auto accident. Then it came to her in a rush that he was talking about *Libby's* life, not hers.

Libby's mother had found her husband in a compromising position with her best friend and promptly filed for divorce. Though Stella never seemed to mind, the publicity had been hard on Libby.

"Some men aren't meant to be parents," was all Sierra could think to say.

"And some women aren't, either," Matt added. "Now about the party — I'll pick you up at eight."

Although the event did sound like fun, especially with Matt on her arm, Sierra refused to abandon common sense and succumb to masculine charm. "I'm sorry —"

"Your mother is the principal backer of the Advocacy Center," Matt interrupted her, an extra measure of persuasiveness now in his tone. "But it's an expensive project. The more money that can be raised the better."

"What does any of that have to do with the party?"

"It's not just a party," Matt said. "It's a fund-raiser for the Advocacy Center. There'll be a silent auction. Many of the Center's proponents will be there hoping to convince some well-known Santa Barbara philanthropists to ante up."

Sierra drew her eyebrows together. "I thought Stella, um, my mother was putting up the money?"

"She's financing the start-up costs," Matt said. "But ongoing support will still be needed if the Center is going to remain viable five and ten years down the road."

Normally Sierra would jump at the chance to solicit funds for such a worthy project. But what if there was someone Libby knew in attendance? Granted, Libby had never been one to indulge in the Santa Barbara social scene and Stella Carlyle had never considered herself part of the community. . . .

"Could you get me a guest list?" Sierra asked impulsively, wondering why she just didn't say no.

"Why?"

"I'd like to see if they've left anyone off

that should be invited," she said, quickly improvising.

"Will you go if I get you the list?" Matt asked immediately.

"If you get me the list, I'll be very grateful," Sierra answered, sidestepping the question.

"Consider it done," he said. "I'll get it from Jim in the morning then I'll stop by the shop and drop it off."

"Perfect." Sierra would connect with Libby tomorrow and show her the names. And, regardless of what she'd insinuated to Matt, her attendance at the party would depend entirely on Libby's response. "I'll be in about eleven."

"I'll see you then," he said. "And, Sierra?"

Her gaze drifted to the clock and she widened her eyes. How in the world was she ever going to get up and have Maddie to play group on time? "Yes, Matt?"

"Most women find me irresistible in a tux," he said in a confident tone. "So Friday night . . ."

"Yes?" she said a trifle impatiently.

"I have two words for you."

She heaved a frustrated sigh. "And what two words would that be?"

"Be prepared."

Matt straightened the jacket of his tux and stole a quick glance at his watch before returning his gaze to the voluptuous brunette. She'd been chattering nonstop since she'd cornered him a few minutes ago, but at the moment he couldn't recall a single word she'd said.

James Hanna's large house with windows overlooking the Pacific was a perfect setting for the party. Music from a small chamber orchestra provided a pleasant backdrop to the guests' chatter and the sweet scent of the exotic flowers brought in just for the occasion, filled the air. The buffet tables brimmed with trays of delicious hors d'oeuvres and the wine that filled the glass in his hand was top-notch.

For the past hour, Matt had mingled, always keeping one eye on the door. He told himself that he was just interested in the attendees, but the truth was he was looking for the pretty blonde who'd assured him she would meet him by the front door promptly at eight. It was now almost nine and Sierra was nowhere in sight.

He blew out a frustrated breath wishing he'd insisted on picking her up. But when he'd suggested it, she'd balked. At the time he'd been so glad she'd agreed to go with him that he'd simply said okay. Now he had to wonder if even back then she'd planned to stand him up.

"Why did I even go to all the work of getting that guest list if she wasn't going to show?" Matt muttered, feeling his anger mount with each passing second.

"Pardon me?"

Matt blinked, only then realizing that Missy or Mindy, or whatever her name was, still stood before him.

"Did you say something?" she asked in a deliberately husky voice designed to stir a man's senses.

Though she was an attractive woman and he'd once favored brunettes, her beauty left his senses untouched. The only thing he could figure was that his tastes were changing.

He almost blew her off, but good manners won out and he offered a conciliatory smile. "I was just commenting on your story."

Actually he hadn't been listening at all. He'd heard the first part — something about a recent trip to Greece — and had immediately tuned her out.

"Silly me," she said, gazing up at him through lowered lashes. "I thought you invited me to a show."

Matt groaned. Of all the women in the room, why did she have to be James Hanna's niece? James was a big deal in Santa Barbara and he'd talked about using Dixon and Associates for his firm's legal work.

Still, the last thing Matt wanted was to take Mitzi on a date. Thankfully, he had a ready excuse.

"You must have misunderstood," he offered her a mollifying smile. "Not that I don't find you attractive but I'm seeing someone."

For a second the woman's face fell, but it only took a second for her to regain her composure. She glanced around the room. "Is your girlfriend here?"

"Not yet," Matt said, resisting the urge to look at his watch again. "But I'm expecting her any minute."

"If you were mine, I wouldn't let you out of my sight for even one second." She took a step closer and the overpowering scent of her expensive perfume wafted over him. "Temptation is everywhere."

Her hand moved to his arm and she gazed up at him questioningly.

Matt realized ruefully that temptation wasn't just everywhere, it was right in front of him dressed in a low-cut black gown. She was an attractive package, he'd give her that, but the trouble was, she wasn't the woman he wanted tonight.

He mouthed some vague excuse about seeing someone he knew and made a hasty retreat, his gaze still firmly fixed on the door.

By ten o'clock, he'd given up hope and his anger soared. He was almost tempted to look up Mitzi and take her up on her offer. But even as the thought entered his mind, Matt rejected it. He'd never used a woman like that before and he wasn't going to start now.

By eleven o'clock, worry replaced anger. Sierra had promised she'd attend and though he didn't know her well, she seemed the reliable sort.

He'd tried to call her home phone several times but all he'd gotten was the recorder. Crazy thoughts ran through his head. What if she were sick? What if she'd been in an accident?

If he knew where she lived he'd drive over there and make sure she was all right. Unfortunately, he didn't have her home address and she'd told him once she wasn't in the phone book.

He thought for a moment. His father

would know her address. After all, Sierra lived in her mother's old house and his dad had been there many times. Matt moved to the outside deck and hit speed dial.

It rang several times before his father answered. "Hello, Matt."

By the sounds of the laughter and clinking glasses in the background, Matt concluded his father was out "being seen." When Dix had been told by his doctor to cut back his workload, his father had decided to use his recuperation time to full advantage and increase his visibility at prominent social events.

It had been a smart move, and had already generated an impressive amount of new clients and an even more impressive revenue spike.

"I need a favor," Matt said. "Do you have Stella Carlyle's home address?"

"She lives just outside of Paris," his father said. "But I don't have the address with me and I'm in the middle of something right now —"

"Actually, it's her address in Santa Barbara that I need," Matt said quickly, not giving his father a chance to finish or to hang up. "Her daughter and I were supposed to meet at a party tonight and we must have got our wires crossed. I just wanted to stop by her place and make sure she's okay."

"Stella's daughter?" A spark of interest sounded in his father's voice. "Are you and Elizabeth Carlyle involved?"

The blatant approval in his father's voice took Matt by surprise.

"Involved might be too strong a word," Matt hedged.

His father no longer seemed in such a hurry to get off the phone. "Is she as pretty as her mother?"

"She's blond." Matt hoped Sierra wasn't lying on her floor in need of medical attention while he was wasting time exchanging inane comments with his father. Still, past experience had taught him, it did no good to rush his dad.

"Ditzy?"

"No, she's not. And that's why I'm concerned. It's not like her not to show." Matt heaved an exasperated sigh. "Do you have the address or not?"

"Let me think." Silence filled the phone lines for several long heartbeats. "I don't have the address but I can give you directions. The house is an old Victorian just off Santa Barbara Street on Arrellaga. Tall hedges all around. You can't miss it."

Matt pictured the area in his mind.

Arrellaga was close to downtown. He calculated the time it would take to get there. Not long, if he caught the lights and drove over the speed-limit.

"Thanks," Matt said. "I appreciate the help."

"Just one question," Dix interjected, before Matt could click off. "Do you like the girl?"

Matt thought for a moment. "At this moment I'd like to throttle her. Does that count?"

His father's robust laugh resounded over the phone lines. "Tells me all I need to know."

The dial tone sounded and Matt swore softly. He was glad someone found this whole situation amusing because he didn't.

Not for one minute.

Chapter Ten

Sierra popped a leftover chocolate petit four into her mouth and sighed. Her mother really did fabulous things with pastries.

Grabbing a dishrag, Sierra moved to the refrigerator surface for a final touch-up. She glanced up at the clock on Libby's kitchen wall.

Almost midnight. If she were Cinderella, she'd be just about to turn back into a scullery maid.

Glancing down at her faded blue jeans and well-washed UC Santa Barbara Gauchos T-shirt, Sierra smiled ruefully. Tonight she didn't need to change back because she'd never gotten to be a princess. Despite her best intentions and a new dress, she'd ending up chucking her plans and staying home to help her mother.

If only I hadn't stopped by Libby's house . . .

After dropping Maddie off for an overnight play date with a friend, Sierra had swung by Libby's to borrow some shoes. Instead of some sleek black pumps, she'd found her mother and Libby in the kitchen frantically trying to fill a last-minute order.

In addition to being Libby's house-keeper, Peggy Summers also ran her own up-and-coming catering service. Business had really taken off right before last Christmas and the hectic pace had continued into the summer. Usually Sierra worked side by side with her mother but since she and Libby had switched places, assisting with the catering had become Libby's responsibility. Unfortunately this last-minute crisis demanded far more than just two sets of hands.

Apparently the original caterer had backed out at the last minute, leaving the hostess in the lurch. The frantic woman had offered Peggy twice the going rate if she could step in. Though Libby let Peggy use her kitchen any time she needed it, Sierra's mother had been hoping to save enough money to one day have her own catering facility. The income from this job would go a long way toward helping Peggy achieve that goal.

That's why Sierra had pulled on an apron and pitched in without even being asked. By eleven, they were in good shape for the next day's event.

Libby had been exhausted and Sierra had sent her to bed, saying one person could easily do the rest of the clean-up. Her mother, who'd have to be up at dawn tomorrow, had offered to stay but Sierra had sent her home, too.

Sierra didn't mind the job or working alone. She'd always enjoyed taking something messy and making it shiny and new again. In fact, she'd probably had more fun spending the evening in the kitchen than she'd have had at the party, even with a handsome man at her side.

She stilled and the dishrag in her hand paused on the chrome finish of the refrigerator door.

I never called Matt.

Guilt swept over her. She'd promised she'd be at the front door of James Hanna's house at eight. But she'd gotten so involved in helping her mother, she'd completely forgotten about the party. Her gaze slid to the clock.

It was too late to call now.

Too late to apologize.

Too late to find out firsthand what he'd meant by "be prepared."

For a second she let herself imagine a different kind of evening. Instead of being elbow deep in flour, she'd have been in Matt's arms. They would have laughed and danced and talked. He would have plied her with outrageous compliments that she wouldn't have believed for a minute but that still would have made her feel all warm and gooey inside.

She'd have talked to people about the Center and they'd all have been enthusiastic and ready to open their wallets. The evening would have been a roaring success. Afterward Matt would have walked her to her car and kissed her until her head whirled. Then, like Cinderella, the clock would have struck twelve and she'd have gone home.

The thought brought her back to the present with a start and she snorted back a laugh. Matt Dixon was no Prince Charming. And, she was certainly no Cinderella.

Sierra finished wiping the refrigerator, gave the countertops another once-over and smiled in satisfaction. Seeing it now, you could never tell all the work that had gone on here this evening. Except . . .

Her gaze critically scanned the small kitchen rug at the base of the sink. It might be only her imagination but it looked like the tiny oval could benefit from a good shaking.

She stared a moment longer but, try as she might, Sierra couldn't convince herself to leave this one last detail unattended. Picking up the rug, she folded it in half and went outside, making sure not even one speck of lint fell on Libby's polished hardwood floors.

The veranda drew her like a magnet. The wide expanse of wood had once been her and Libby's play area. When they were young, they'd draped blankets over the railing and made forts. When they were older the porch had been the place where she and Libby had perfected animal calls.

Sierra chuckled to herself, remembering the first time they'd demonstrated their newfound talent in front of Stella. They'd been about nine at the time and Libby had gone first, doing a fairly respectable chicken squawk. Sierra had followed with her version of a pig's oink. Unlike Libby, who'd refused to flap her wings as they'd practiced, Sierra had taken a finger and lifted her nose so it resembled a pig's snout and let loose with the loudest oink she could muster.

Libby's mom had been clearly stunned by the realistic sounds. She didn't applaud, but instead raised one perfectly arched eyebrow, and told them Peggy had cookies waiting for them inside on the dining-room table.

Sierra gave a melancholy sigh. Those were the good old days. Though she knew she should lock up and head home to bed, she couldn't bring herself to move. It was a beautiful evening and the first time she'd had a chance to relax all day. The temperature hovered around sixty-five and the air was fresh with only the faintest hint of moisture. Sierra shook the rug then draped it carefully over the railing. Resting her elbows on the soft fibers, she leaned forward and stared out into the darkness.

Life had been so simple then. It hadn't taken much to bring happiness: chocolate-chip cookies, a good book and a loud oink.

Sierra's lips turned up in a smile. She hadn't oinked in forever. At one time she'd been quite good. She wondered if it was like riding a bike, once you learned, you never forgot? Or was it like the French she'd learned in middle school? She'd never used it and now the only thing she could do was count to ten.

Of course, there was one way to find out. . . .

Straightening to make sure she had the support of her diaphragm, Sierra put her finger to her nose and let out a big, bad oink. The shrill squeal split the air and down the block a dog barked in response.

Sierra smiled, pleased that she hadn't lost her touch.

"Is that why you skipped the party?" The deep voice came from the shadows at the bottom of the steps. "So you could practice barnyard sounds?"

Sierra's heart leaped to her throat and she grasped the railing to steady herself. "Matt. What are you doing here?"

Matt had come from the other side of the house only minutes before and caught sight of her standing on the veranda. His initial reaction had been relief; at least she wasn't lying unconscious somewhere. The next was anger; she *had* stood him up.

The temptation had been strong to call out to her, but he'd resisted the impulse, waiting first to see if she was alone.

When no one appeared, he'd started toward her, only to stop dead in his tracks at the ungodly sound splitting the night air.

"What was that?" Matt gazed up at her from the steps leading to the porch. "It sounded just like a pig."

"It *did* sound pretty realistic." Sierra's smile widened and pride filled her voice. "I guess it is like riding a bike — once you've mastered the technique you've got it for life."

Matt ignored the comment and climbed the stairs, not waiting for an invitation. "It's too bad California isn't a big hog-calling state, or you could have a real career in front of you."

Her gaze narrowed and suspicion filled her eyes. "Are you teasing me?"

"Maybe." He found it impossible to keep from smiling. "That sound really threw me for a loop."

Sierra's lips curved upward in an answering smile. "We all need to be thrown off course once in a while."

She looked so beautiful when she smiled that for a moment he could only stare. She didn't need to be wearing an elegant evening gown to take his breath away. He paused, suddenly remembering why he was here. "About tonight —"

"I'm sorry about standing you up." She gathered up the rug and shot him an apologetic glance. "How about I explain everything over a cup of cocoa?"

"Cocoa?"

"With marshmallows," she added. "The real stuff. Not from a box."

He shrugged and nodded, struck again by how lovely she looked in the moonlight. Her hair resembled spun gold and her eyes were wide and luminous. Her T-shirt and jeans accentuated her lean, curvy figure and sent his pulses racing.

"Take a seat." She gestured with one hand to two chairs that flanked a rustic table. "I'll be back in a jiffy."

In a jiffy?

Matt shook his head, sauntered to the table and sat down. He leaned back and loosened his tie. Maybe he'd lied to his dad. Maybe Elizabeth Carlyle was a little bit ditzy. And maybe he was a little crazy for finding her so attractive.

True to her word, she returned several minutes later with two steaming mugs.

"Enjoy." Sierra placed a cup before him, took her own and sat down.

The smell of rich chocolate mixed with the sweet scent of rapidly melting marshmallows tempted his taste buds. Though he'd always associated the drink with cold weather and roaring fires, he decided to give it a try.

"Delicious," he admitted after taking a sip.

Sierra favored him with a smile. "My mother always said I made the best hot chocolate."

Matt took another sip. Based on how his father had described Stella, he was surprised the woman even knew what a kitchen was, much less encouraged her daughter's culinary endeavors.

"Don't tell me you like to cook?" Try as he might, Matt couldn't keep the surprise from his voice.

"Very much." Sierra nodded and took a sip of her own cocoa. A trace of the sticky sweetness coated her lips and she reached for her napkin.

But Matt was quicker. His fingers curved over hers and he plucked the napkin from her hand. "Allow me."

Sierra smiled and puckered her lips.

Matt groaned. He'd wanted to talk things out before he kissed her, but nothing about this night was going as planned.

He dropped the napkin to the table, leaned forward and covered her mouth with his.

Matt had intended it to be a brief kiss. But the moment his lips met hers, all lucid thoughts fled. And when her hand traveled up his arm to his shoulder and her fingers slipped through the hair at the nape of his neck, the only thing that mattered was her.

Her lips were warm. Gentle fingers caressed his neck, making his heart beat hard and fast. When she started to pull away, he wanted nothing more than to crush her to him.

"I've missed kissing you." Sierra sighed as his mouth left hers, a soft regretful sigh that nudged at his already tenuous control.

"It seems like years," he said.

Sierra stared at him, her eyes large and luminous in the moonlight. "I'm thinking this could be a hard habit to break."

Matt smiled. He'd learned long ago that some habits weren't worth breaking. It was all he could do not to pull her to him and convince her of that fact. But first, the question of why she'd stood him up needed to be answered.

But when her fingers laced through his hair and she lifted her face for another kiss, Matt decided it didn't matter where she'd been, all that mattered was that she was here with him now.

Her breath fell outward on a soft sigh as his mouth covered hers. She tasted of marshmallow and chocolate, a sweet combination. He felt her hands lower to grip the lapels of his tux.

Matt angled his head and deepened the kiss.

Her lips parted and he unhurriedly claimed her mouth. They kissed for what seemed like forever and only when his hands tugged impatiently at the soft cotton of her T-shirt, pulling it loose from the waistband of her jeans, did she jerk back and push his hands away.

He met her gaze. "Let me stay with you tonight."

Though the look in her eyes told him she was sorely tempted, she shook her head. "That can't happen."

"I don't have to stay all night," Matt said. "That's something we can decide later."

He moved toward her but Sierra stepped back and shifting her gaze downward, methodically tucked her shirt into the waistband of her jeans. When she looked up, Matt knew he was in trouble by the coolness in her eyes.

"Do you really want to spend the night with someone you barely know?" she asked.

He stared at her for a long moment, contemplating the best way to answer such a tricky question.

"I like you," he said, finally.

Sierra tilted her head. "What is it you like about me?"

"First another kiss." He trailed a finger up the bare skin of her arm. "All this talking is making me hungry."

Sierra smiled and Matt's hopes rose once, only to plummet when she removed his hand from her arm with a firm, deliberate gesture. "First we talk."

Matt blew out a frustrated breath. There were so many things he liked about her that they'd be talking all night if he mentioned them all. And *talking* wasn't what he wanted to be doing right now. "You're upbeat and funny, not to mention incredibly beautiful."

"But what about my views on current events, religion, politics?" she asked, returning his smile.

Matt shrugged.

"For all you know I could be a socialist," she added.

"For all you know, I could be one," he said, hoping to tease her out of this obsessive need to talk everything to death.

"Matt," she said, a hint of warning in her tone.

"C'mon, Sierra." He reached forward and took her hand, his thumb caressing her palm. "Don't be so obstinate."

"Obstinate?" She jerked back her hand.

The minute her voice rose and her eyes flashed, Matt knew it'd been the wrong thing to say.

She lifted her chin. "I'm obstinate because I won't fall into bed with you?"

Matt groaned to himself. Why did she keep saying they'd just met? They'd known each other now for what seemed like weeks. And their parents had known each other for years. It wasn't as if they were strangers. "I don't want to do that, either."

Sierra lifted a skeptical eyebrow.

"I feel a connection with you," he admitted.

"How can you feel a connection with someone you just met?" she asked.

"We didn't just meet," he said emphasizing each word through gritted teeth. "Anyway, there's more to feeling connected than knowing someone's voting record. Take Carl for example. Would you say he knows you?"

"What does he have to do with this?"

"Humor me," Matt said.

"Okay, yes, he knows me," Sierra said.

"And you know him?" Matt persisted. "You know his feelings on politics, current events, religion?"

"I've listened to a lot of sermons," she said. "I've been in his Bible Study groups. And his views on the major issues are clear."

"But you still don't want to kiss him."

Sierra frowned. "I've told you before

that I'm not attracted to Carl. Not in that way."

"But you are to me," he said triumphantly.

"I don't see the point," Sierra said.

"It doesn't matter how long or how well you know someone," Matt said. "When you're talking about being connected, what matters is the chemistry."

"Chemistry is part of it, but not all," Sierra insisted. "You have to know what makes someone tick to feel truly close to them. Chemistry alone can't sustain a relationship."

Matt stared at her for a long moment, realizing finally that she was going to make this as difficult as possible. "Have I told you that I'm deeply committed to preserving the environment? Or that I'm not a Socialist. I'm actually an Independent. And, in case you're wondering about church affiliation, I'm a member of Brentwood Christian."

The lines of concentration deepened along her eyebrows and under her eyes. "Matt, that kind of information is fine and dandy, but it's not enough."

"That was preliminary," he said quickly. "If there's anything else you want to know, just ask."

"I can ask anything?" The assessing look in her eye took him by surprise.

"Anything that's not protected by attorney-client privilege," he said.

"Hmm." A finger rose to her lips and she thought for a moment.

His sense of unease increased with each passing second but he told himself he was being foolish. After all, she'd probably just ask the same old questions all women asked. Things like what was his birthday? His favorite food or color? What was his favorite sports team? The possibilities were endless.

Sierra took another sip of cocoa and leaned back, her fingers embracing the mug. "What was it like when your mother left?"

Chapter Eleven

What was it like? What did she think it was like?

Matt picked up the mug in front of him and took a big drink. The hot cocoa seared his throat, but he relished the pain. Obviously, Sierra didn't realize he never talked about that time in his life. Not to Tori, not to his father, not to anyone.

He thought about telling her it was too personal, or that it was none of her business, but then he remembered his promise. He'd always been a man of his word, so he'd answer her question. But he'd keep it short and sweet.

"It was hard. One day she was there. The next she was gone." He relayed the events as if he was an impartial observer. "My sister cried herself to sleep for months. My dad buried himself in his work."

"And you?" she prompted.

"I did the best I could to comfort my sister." The memory of Tori's heartbreak stood vivid in his mind. "And to stay out of my dad's way."

His father had said something to the effect of "good riddance to bad rubbish" but Matt knew his mother's leaving had hit him hard. Not only had she taken a good chunk of his bank account with her, she'd left him with two kids he barely knew.

"You were there for your sister." Sierra placed a hand on his arm. "Who was there for you?"

"I did okay on my own." He'd been strong and had taken her leaving like a man, as his father had instructed.

But there'd been nights, when he was sure no one would overhear, that he'd cried. And as angry as he'd been at her for leaving, he still missed her. Missed the way she tousled his hair and called him "sport." Missed the way she sang silly songs in the car. But, most of all, he missed the way she used to hug him and say she loved him, even when he tried to pull away.

Even now his heart clenched, remembering.

"When my father left," Sierra said, "my faith was a real blessing."

"Our minister came over after my mother took off, but he and my father got into an argument. Dad told him that you can only count on yourself," Matt said. "Said this was a prime example why a person shouldn't put their faith in anyone but themselves. Needless to say, the pastor didn't agree."

"What do you believe?" Sierra asked softly.

Matt steeled his heart against the compassion in her voice. Though he'd always believed there was no value in rehashing the past, it felt good to talk about that time. Especially with someone like Sierra who listened rather than telling him what he should think or feel.

"I believe that most of the time, given the chance, people will disappoint you," Matt said.

An odd look crossed her face and he wondered if he should have been so honest. For a second he thought she was going to argue the point. Instead, she took another sip of cocoa. "Do you see your mother now?"

"I haven't seen her since the day she walked out the door," Matt said. "What really galls me is now she thinks she can come back, say she's sorry and —"

Matt stopped short, realizing too late that he'd said too much. But those blasted letters from her kept coming and though he told himself he should just throw them into the trash unread, he couldn't bring himself to do that. Not after all those years of checking the mailbox every day, hoping she'd written.

"You can't forgive her."

"She doesn't deserve to be forgiven," Matt said flatly.

"Grace is something *needed* but not *deserved*," Sierra said, and he found himself wondering if they were just words or if she really believed them. "We didn't deserve to be forgiven, but God forgave us. Can we do any less for others?"

It was ironic, Matt thought, that the things that were so hard in life always sounded so simple. He fixed his gaze on Sierra. "Have you forgiven the man who hurt you?"

Sierra lowered her gaze to the mug on the table and after a long moment, shook her head.

"Then you understand," he said in a low tone, "how hard it can be to do the right thing."

"I do." Sierra sighed. "And I'm beginning to realize that you and I have more in common than I thought."

"That's good," Matt said.

"I'm not so sure," Sierra murmured.

The sentiment took Matt by surprise. He frowned. "I thought that you wanted to get to know me."

"I did," she said. "But somehow I thought I'd like you less, not more."

The tightness that had gripped Matt's shoulders eased and his lips curved upward in a smug smile. "I knew you liked me."

"Arrogant jerk," she shot back, but there was no rancor in her tone.

"Piggy." Matt chuckled and said it a couple more times for good measure. "Piggy. Piggy."

Sierra's eyes widened. "What did you call me?"

"Piggy," he repeated, his mood lightening by the minute.

Her gaze narrowed.

"Hey, I find oinking incredibly attractive," he added.

She rolled her eyes and laughed. "Why does it not surprise me that you found a way to steer the conversation back to our little problem?"

He shot her a wink. "Babe, when I'm with you, I can't think of much else."

She paused for a long moment then leaned forward and rested her arms on the tabletop. "Don't you see that jumping into an intimate relationship would be settling for less than you deserve?"

Matt stifled a groan. He'd had enough of the heavy conversation for one evening.

"Don't you want to save such intimacy for someone who loves you? Someone you can trust? Someone who has pledged before God to be by your side forever?"

Matt's eyebrows pulled together. "You're talking marriage?"

Sierra nodded.

"Marriage is a wonderful concept," he said. "But if you think saying vows in a church means that someone will always be there for you, I'm here to tell you it just ain't so. People bail on their spouses and children every day."

"I could never leave my child," Sierra said vehemently. "Never."

"But what about a husband?" Matt kept his tone even. "Can you sit there and tell me that no matter what, if you married someone you'd never leave him?"

"There are certain circumstances —"

"Then you agree that marriage and a ring on your finger doesn't guarantee anything," Matt said wishing they were both a little less cynical.

Sierra shifted her gaze out over the darkened yard. When she'd married Jerry, she intended it to be forever. But she couldn't remain with a man who not only didn't respect his marriage vows, but who could hurt his own child.

But Matt was right about one thing. In the end, all the promises she and Jerry had made in front of God on that beautiful June day meant nothing.

"You're right," Sierra said, unable to stem the wave of sadness washing over her. "There are no guarantees."

"We're thinking too much." Matt leaned forward and took her hand. "How about we just enjoy the moment?" Despite the shiver that traveled up her spine at Matt's touch, Sierra refused to go down that road.

"I'm afraid I'm not a live-in-the-moment kind of gal." Though she knew she was making the right decision, Sierra couldn't keep a twinge of regret from her tone. "I'm the ring-on-my-finger-before-intimacy type."

"You want to get married?"

The shocked look on Matt's face made her laugh.

"Someday," Sierra said, waving one hand dismissively in the air. "Not now. And, you don't have a thing to worry about. I'm definitely not out to marry you."

"Why not?" Instead of being relieved that she wasn't on a manhunt with him in her sights, he sounded affronted. "I've been told by some that I'm considered a good catch."

"I'm sure you are," Sierra murmured. "For the right woman."

"But not you?"

Sierra shrugged.

"I know how to cook spaghetti," Matt said. "And I make great garlic bread."

Sierra couldn't help but laugh. "You're such a brat."

"And you're such a piggy," he answered.

She didn't know what made her do it. Impulsively she opened her mouth and oinked.

But he didn't laugh as she'd expected. Instead, his eyes darkened and he leaned close. So close she could see the flecks of gold in his eyes and smell the enticing scent of his cologne.

"I told you what that sound does to me."

Sierra was unable to stop the thrill of excitement that raced through her at the look in his eyes.

Matt rose and leaned over, pulling her up from her chair with one hand before sitting down and tugging her into his lap. His arms closed around her. "I could kiss you all night."

"You're not spending the night."

"Okay." He nibbled her ear. "Let me rephrase. I could kiss you for hours."

Sierra was glad she was sitting because just the thought made her go weak in the knees.

"If we kiss, you have to promise you'll keep your hands to yourself," she said, inhaling the woodsy scent of his cologne.

"Spoilsport," he said, nuzzling her neck.

Her breath caught in her throat. "All we do is kiss."

His only response was to lift his head and shift his attention back to her ear. "You certainly have a lot of requests," he murmured, moving from her ear to scatter kisses along her jawline. "Good thing I'm an understanding guy."

"Understanding?" she asked, catching her breath.

The hand at her neck urged her to him, and warm, sweet lips brushed her mouth. "It's just one of my many virtues."

His hands moved on her shoulders, caressing against her shirt, his palms learning the softness of her upper arms, his thumbs following the delicacy of her collarbone.

Sierra's breath caught in her throat and Matt chuckled, his arms encircling her, pulling T-shirt against tux. What she and Matt had was pure physical attraction. It wasn't a forever kind of thing.

But Sierra would revel in every blissful moment.

Until the summer ended and he was gone.

Chapter Twelve

"My life is a lot like fraternizing with the enemy," Sierra told Libby three weeks later when the two met for lunch.

Libby's fork dropped into her mandarin-orange salad and a look of alarm filled her gaze. "Jerry is stalking you?"

It took Sierra a second to figure out why Libby would make such an off-the-wall comment. Once she did, she had to laugh. "I'm not talking about Jerry."

And, actually Jerry was the last thing Sierra wanted to think about, much less discuss. She'd received another "forgive me" message on her voice mail this morning and only by sheer will had she kept from letting it ruin her day.

Libby exhaled an audible breath. "Then what are you talking about?"

"Matt and I." The moment the words were spoken she realized how second nature they'd become. In the past few weeks she and Matt had become an item; going to movies, meeting for lunch at the park, hammering out details related to the Advocacy Center over dinner. And kissing until her senses reeled. "I feel so guilty."

Libby's blue eyes widened and she leaned forward. When she spoke her voice was so low, Sierra could barely hear the question. "Are you telling me you finally gave in to him?"

"No, I wouldn't do that," Sierra said a trifle impatiently. "I just meant that hanging out with Matt is like hanging out with your enemy."

"You and he seem pretty tight for enemies," Libby observed.

That was the problem, Sierra thought. Every day they grew closer. She enjoyed talking to him, visiting about his day, telling him about hers.

"We have fun," Sierra said. "But every so often I have to pinch myself and remember that he's Lawrence Dixon's son."

Libby shrugged. "Everybody is somebody's son. And when you think about it, Dix was only doing his job."

"Matt isn't a believer," Sierra said. "And you know how important that is to me."

"Correct me if I'm wrong," Libby said. "But haven't you two gone to church together the last few weeks and didn't you tell me that he's agreed to go to the Praise Festival this weekend?"

"What does that have to do with any-thing?" Sierra said.

"Maybe he and God are back on good terms," Libby said. "Why else would he agree to go?"

"I don't know," Sierra said.

"Maybe you need to ask him," Libby said. "You two need to do more than just kiss when you're together."

Despite her friend's teasing tone Sierra could feel her face warm in a guilty flush. "We do talk."

Libby laughed, clearly enjoying her friend's discomfort. "Then talk about things that are important to you. Talk about his faith. See where he stands."

Sierra exhaled a breath. While Matt had more than once tried to steer the conversation around to more serious topics she'd been the one intent on keeping things light. "I suppose I could ask."

"What about kids?" Libby asked. "Does he like kids?"

"I'm not sure," Sierra said. "I don't re-call us seeing many children when we're together."

"That's cuz you were too busy kissing to notice," Libby said with an impish smile.

"Shut up." Sierra chuckled. "You and Carson do your share of locking lips, and don't tell me different."

"True." Libby's gaze turned dreamy. "He's a great kisser."

"Are you two talking about the future?"

Like Sierra, her friend had gone into this summer romance with her boss with a no-strings-attached understanding. But lately Sierra had sensed a change.

"Not really," Libby said.

"That's because you spend too much time kissing," Sierra teased.

Libby burst our laughing. "Point taken."

"You ladies look like you're having a good time."

Sierra's head jerked in the direction of the familiar voice, her heart automatically picking up speed.

Matt stood next to the table, looking positively delectable in a pair of worn blue jeans and a plain white shirt that did wonderful things for his tan.

"Doesn't look like you're working today," Sierra observed, the inane comment giving her the time she needed to recover her balance which had been unexpectedly rocked by the sight of him standing there, his blue eyes a little sleepy, his dark hair appealingly tousled, and all of him blatantly, appealingly masculine.

He smiled, showing a mouthful of perfect white teeth. "I was up late working on some cases and slept in. I stopped by the store to see if you wanted to go to lunch, but Dottie told me you'd already left."

His gaze shifted to Libby and he smiled, clearly appreciating Libby's beauty.

A faint stirring of what felt like jealousy rose up in Sierra, but she shoved it down. She had no claim on Matt.

"I don't believe we've ever met," Matt stuck out his hand. "Matt Dixon."

"Libby Summers," Libby said, taking his hand. "It's a pleasure."

Libby cast Sierra an apologetic glance. "I'm afraid I need to rush. Carson gets cranky if I take too long."

"Carson?" Matt asked.

"My boss." Libby rolled her eyes. "I work at the Waterfront and he thinks an hour and a half is more than enough time for lunch."

Sierra smiled. Libby always made it sound like she worked for a slave driver. But Sierra had met Carson. Not only was he nice, but Sierra thought his request that Libby be on time in the morning and limit her lunch hour to ninety minutes was perfectly reasonable.

"Are you a waitress?" Matt asked.

"I tried, but it was a disaster," Libby said

with a rueful laugh. "Now I'm stuck doing payroll and scheduling. Boring with a capital *B*."

"I'm currently interviewing receptionists for our Santa Barbara office," Matt said. "If you're interested I —"

"Thanks, but don't worry about me," Libby said, her brilliant smile softening the refusal. Her gaze lowered to her watch and she yelped and jumped to her feet. "I didn't realize it was *this* late. If I don't get going now, I might need another job."

"If you change your mind," Matt called after her, "let Sierra know."

"Thanks," Libby called back, clattering down the walk in her high-heeled sandals.

Sierra shook her head. Libby somehow always managed to look cool and elegant no matter what the circumstance.

"Now that I've scared your luncheon companion off," Matt said, with that smile that made her heart do flip-flops, "mind if I join you?"

Sierra smiled and gestured to Libby's empty chair. "Please do."

Though she'd enjoyed her lunch with Libby, Sierra found she rather liked the curious humming excitement that now coursed through her.

The waiter brought Matt a menu and

while he studied it, Sierra's gaze shifted to the tourists ambling down State Street, children and shopping bags in hand.

Her gaze fixed on a father with a preschool-age boy and a girl about seven. The man stood on the sidewalk, just outside of the restaurant's cordoned-off area furiously digging in his pockets. Given the rapidly melting cones that each child held, Sierra guessed the dad was searching for a napkin.

Sierra cringed. Any mother knew you should never get a double-dip in this heat. There was no way a small child could eat it fast enough to keep it from dripping. And even with a single, the napkins had to be in hand and ready to wipe.

Matt noticed Sierra staring and followed the direction of her gaze. Though they were built completely differently and didn't look at all the same, the man reminded Matt of his father. Dix was a master in the courtroom but put him in charge of a couple of kids and he was clueless.

"Look at that guy," Matt said, remembering how frustrated his father would get when their planned "together time" fell apart. "He looks miserable."

Sierra glanced back at the man who'd finally found the elusive napkin. He looked harried as any person facing dripping chocolate would be, but not especially miserable.

"I bet he drives a minivan," Matt mused, remembering how his father had bought one after his mother had left. Dix had hated the vehicle with a passion, though both Matt and Tori had loved it.

"You'll have one, too, someday," Sierra told him. "They're great when you have children."

"If you want kids," Matt said. It had been an automatic comment of his for years, one he said without even thinking anymore. But as the words left his mouth, he realized the sentiment might no longer be accurate.

The more he was around Sierra, the more he found himself wondering what it would be like to have a little boy with her blond hair or a little girl with green eyes. Sierra was so warm and nurturing that he felt certain she would be a good mother. And, maybe, given time, he could learn how to be a good father.

"You don't want children?" Her voice rose with surprise.

Matt realized with his quick response he'd given her the wrong impression, so he qualified his answer. "My own someday,

167

but definitely no stepchildren."

"Really?" Sierra choked on her tea but waved away his offer of a napkin.

"That's a hard road," he said, warming to the topic. "I see it every day in the divorces I handle. It's hard to raise another man's children. That's why I've always made it a point not to date a woman with children."

"Sort of the old, don't date anyone you wouldn't want to marry rule?" Sierra added in a light tone.

Matt nodded, glad it no longer mattered because sitting across from him was the only woman he wanted. One who was perfect for him. "I hadn't really thought of it that way, but it makes sense."

Sierra carefully placed her glass of tea back on the tabletop and tried to ignore the sudden tightness gripping her heart. She told herself it didn't matter what Matt thought of children or even dating a woman with children. Despite a few silly daydreams, she'd always known they'd never be together forever.

"Johnny, listen to me." The father's voice rose in frustration.

Matt and Sierra shifted their gazes at the same time.

The dad still stood in the same place

only now his hand was outstretched holding a napkin. "Wipe your hands."

The cone had disappeared but sticky dark chocolate smears covered the boy's hands and face. When the bright-eyed tow-head raised his hands and stared at them, Sierra could see the writing on the wall.

Smiling broadly, the child wiped his hands down the front of his shirt.

The father groaned and raised his eyes toward the heavens.

The girl giggled.

The little boy beamed in pride. "All clean."

Matt shook his head. "All I can say is I'm glad it's not me."

A week later, Sierra was still thinking of the incident when she stole one last look in Maddie's bedroom. *Okay, so Matt doesn't like kids. What did it matter, anyway?*

Though Sierra had tried to be blasé, the realization had knocked her for a loop. Because somehow, without her realizing how or why, she'd grown incredibly fond of the guy. He could be exasperating and tenacious as a bulldog when he thought he was right, but he could also be funny and kind.

But none of that mattered. She and Maddie were a team. *Love me, love my* daughter was her mantra. On that there would be no compromise.

The ring of the phone jarred Sierra from her reverie and she raced down the hall, determined to get the phone before it woke Maddie.

Sierra grabbed the phone on the fifth ring, her heart pounding from her sprint. "Hello."

"Hello yourself." Matt's familiar voice filled the phone line. "Busy?"

"Not at this moment," she said, trying to catch her breath.

"I want to see you," he said. "I was going to just drop by, but I remembered what you'd said about calling first."

Sierra smiled at the pained tone in his voice. She'd made it clear on more than one occasion that she didn't appreciate unexpected guests. Actually she didn't mind if people dropped over, she just didn't want him to unexpectedly stop over and find Libby occupying the house he thought was hers.

"I'd like to see you," he repeated when she didn't respond.

"I thought we were planning on lunch tomorrow," Sierra said, leaning back against a nearby chair.

"Tomorrow is hours away," he said.

"Matt." Sierra lowered her voice, not wanting to take the chance on waking Maddie. "You can't come over."

"Why not?"

"You just can't."

"Someone is there with you," he said, and she wondered if she just imagined the unexpected hitch in his voice.

"Yes," Sierra said immediately, then caught herself. "I mean no. I mean someone *is* here, but it's not what you're thinking. . . ."

"You don't have to explain," he said, his tone now cool and distant. "You don't owe me anything."

But he was wrong.

She did owe him something.

She owed him the truth.

Chapter Thirteen

"Matt," Sierra's voice softened. "There's no guy here with me. Just a little girl."

Matt breathed a sigh of relief, feeling foolish for even thinking she'd cheat on him. "Why didn't you just tell me you were baby-sitting?"

He wondered if some of the craziness in his head was because of the heavy-duty thinking he'd been doing lately. Though he'd tried to forget them, Sierra's words about forgiveness had kept niggling at him. Until two nights ago when he'd finally broken down and prayed.

He was amazed he knew how until he remembered that at one time prayers had been a regular part of his bedtime ritual.

When his mother had left, his faith had gone with her. He'd hated her for walking away and he hated God for not stopping her. At the time he thought he'd never be able to forgive either one of them.

Grace is something needed but not deserved.

His mother said she wanted his forgiveness and a chance to start over. Though a tiny part of him wanted to say it was too late, Sierra's words had stopped the easy answer.

"Jan is in town," he said.

"Jan?"

"My mother."

He'd recognized her voice immediately when he'd listened to his messages. Apparently she was staying at the Hotel Santa Barbara and wanted to get together. Calling Sierra had been his first thought.

"Have you seen her?"

"Not yet," he said. "She says she wants to see me."

"I'm sure she does," Sierra said softly. "How could anyone not miss you?"

The tight ache in his chest intensified. "Let me come over."

It was as close as he'd ever come to begging, but he needed to talk to her.

A moment of silence filled the line.

"I'm not at the house," she said. "But you can come over here if you want. . . ."

"What's the address?" he asked, grabbing a pencil. He wrote down the street number and name and a few cursory directions. "I'll be there in ten minutes."

"You don't need to rush," she said. "I'll be here."

Though it wasn't that late now, Matt

didn't want to be interrupted by the untimely return of the parents. "When are they due home?"

"Who?"

"The child's parents."

"I'll be here all night," she said finally. "So, like I said, there's no need to hurry."

The words were familiar. "There's no rush," his mother had said on the recorder. "Get back to me when you can."

Had the time come to make that call?

Eighteen years ago Matt had turned his back on God. Still, God had been ready and willing to forgive him.

Could he do any less for his own mother?

The apartment where Sierra was babysitting was in a working-class area of Santa Barbara. Yard space was at a premium as was available parking. Matt finally found a spot on the street just down the block.

He climbed the stairs to the second-story unit, made sure he had the right number and rapped lightly on the door.

Though she was fully dressed in a pair of shorts and a T-shirt, Sierra looked as if she was ready for bed. Her face had been scrubbed clean of makeup and her feet were bare.

She opened the door wide and motioned him in.

"We're going to have to keep our voices down," she said in a low tone. "So we don't wake up the little one."

Impulsively Matt leaned over and brushed a kiss across her lips as he walked into the living room.

Her cheeks turned a dusky pink. "What was that for?"

Matt almost said, "Because I love you," but stopped himself just in time. He'd only recently realized the depth of his feelings and hadn't yet shared that realization with her. Though he was almost positive she felt the same way, he wanted to be certain. "Because I've missed you."

The living room was neat and clean with a huge trunk of toys in one corner. A tiny kitchen was immediately adjacent to the room with a tiny eating area and breakfast bar.

"Cute place," Matt said, more for conversation's sake than with any real admiration. He gazed at the sofa and chair and then at the kitchen table.

Sierra moved to the sofa and plopped down. She patted a spot beside her. "Come and sit by me."

Matt didn't wait for a second invitation

and when he sat down beside her, his arm automatically moved around her shoulders.

For a long moment he just sat there, reveling in the closeness. She smelled like cherries and he wondered if it was a new perfume or if she'd been making a pie.

He had to smile at the thought of Stella Carlyle's daughter making a pie. Or even baby-sitting. Sierra was just not what he'd expected.

Instead of making conversation, she snuggled against him, so close he could feel her heart beating. He thought of all the times he'd held her close, all the times they'd kissed. All the times he'd pressured her to go further. Shame filled Matt.

The past few weekends he and Sierra had attended church together. She hadn't wanted to go to First Christian since Carl would be there, so they'd gone "church hopping."

It was during one of those Sunday mornings, sitting in the pew beside her and sharing a hymnal that he'd first realized he'd loved her. And with it came the knowledge that he didn't want her for just a night, or a week, or a month, he wanted her with him forever. He wanted her to be his wife and the mother of his children.

Matt realized he'd been wrong to pressure her to be intimate. If she'd given in to his demands, it would have shortchanged them both. He still wanted to make love to her but when they did, she would be his wife and it would be with God's blessing . . . and with the blessings of their family.

His father would be pleased. Matt couldn't count the number of times he'd asked in the past few weeks, if he was still "involved" with Stella's daughter. And, more than once he'd told Matt that he and "Elizabeth" would be a perfect match. He'd gathered from his father that Stella felt the same way.

Matt agreed completely. He and Sierra *were* a match made in heaven.

Though he'd vowed they'd just talk, her closeness stirred his senses. He turned and tilted her face up to his with a crooked finger. "Have I told you lately how much I enjoy your company?"

She shook her head.

"Well, I do," he said. "Very much."

And, suddenly without any plan his lips were closing over hers and his arms were pulling her tight against him.

But this time it was love that was behind the kisses, behind the tender caresses. He took his time kissing her with a leisurely thoroughness that left her breathless. Matt lifted his head slowly, feeling her lips cling to his. Her lashes lay against her skin in soft, sandy crescents for a moment before lifting to reveal a quivering uncertainty.

"Matt, I —"

Matt covered her mouth once more with his, stopping her words. He didn't need her to tell him they wouldn't be going any further tonight, because he'd already decided that, until they were married, kisses were as far as it went.

Still, when he pulled away from her, a deep sigh of regret passed her lips and it gave him solace to know that holding the passion in check was as hard on her as it was on him.

"I really did come here to talk," he said.

She smiled. "I wouldn't have guessed."

"It's just something about sitting on a couch with a pretty girl that makes me feel sixteen again," Matt said, only half joking. He eyed a nearby chair and wondered if he'd be wise to put some distance between them.

She must have noticed the direction of his gaze because she rose with a fluid grace and moved to the chair.

"Maybe this way we can actually talk," she said.

"Worried about me jumping on you?"

"No," she said with an impish smile. "I'm worried about me jumping on you."

He laughed out loud and she shushed him, but he could hear the laughter bubbling up in her own throat.

"Now, what did you want to talk about?"

It was all he could do not to confess his love. Only the determination to have that moment be perfect stopped the words. Instead, he told her about his mother's call and her desire to see him.

They talked for over an hour about his fears and his lingering anger and by the time he left an hour later, Matt felt at peace.

And, as he kissed her one last time at the door, he realized that just when he thought he couldn't love her more, he did.

"Sleep well, sweetheart," he said. "I'll see you tomorrow."

Sierra watched him walk down the hall, only shutting the door when he disappeared from sight.

Sleep well?

Was he kidding?

It'd be a miracle if she slept at all.

"I'm going to tell him the minute he walks up," Sierra told herself for the hundredth time that afternoon. Her mother was watching Maddie so there would be no interruptions.

All day, she'd thought of nothing else but the confession. She had to be honest. This was no longer a silly, summer game where no one would get hurt.

It went without saying that she was going to be hurt. She'd fallen for him. Hard. So, a broken heart was guaranteed.

She suspected he cared for her, too. And the last thing she wanted was for him to be hurt. That's why she had to come clean, before things went any further.

What would he say when she told him? It was possible he would yell and scream the way Jerry used to when he got mad. Sierra dismissed that thought the minute it entered her head. Matt wasn't like Jerry. He rarely even raised his voice.

More than likely, he'd be cool and polite and distant. He'd probably act as though it didn't matter at all. And then, he'd walk out the door and she'd never see him again.

The thought sent a stab of pain straight through her heart and she realized that her mother had once again been right.

She should never have dated a man she didn't want to marry.

Sierra practiced her confession in her head until she was confident she could say the words without stumbling over her tongue. But when she saw him walking up Libby's sidewalk, her mouth went dry and all rational thoughts fled. Striding up the front steps was six feet of solidly muscled, incredibly good-looking male.

She'd told him the Praise Festival was a casual affair and that most of the attendees would be wearing jeans or shorts. Her green-and-gold striped skirt with a sleeveless green-colored top was even probably a little dressy but the newly purchased outfit gave her shaky confidence a boost.

But while she thought she looked quite presentable, Matt looked fabulous. The blue T-shirt emphasized the width of his shoulders and the taut flatness of his stomach. His jeans clung to his lean hips.

Before she could say a word, he was on the porch, pulling her into his arms, his lips closing over hers.

Her arms lifted of their own volition, wrapping around his neck. Her hand fisted as the kiss rushed toward searing. When at last she stepped back, Sierra found herself trembling.

"Was that —" She paused and gave herself a minute to figure out what she was trying to say.

"If you're asking if that was the main course," Matt said with a wink, "it wasn't. That was just an appetizer. I'm saving the best for later."

Later.

The promise whirled in Sierra's mind like an out-of-control top. Would it really be so wrong to wait until they'd gotten the main course out of the way to tell him? After all, why ruin what was promising to be a wonderful evening with the truth?

Chapter Fourteen

The Praise Festival reminded Matt of a cross between a carnival and an old-fashioned community picnic. The area along the sidewalk leading up to the wharf was lined with booths that featured everything from men in suits selling Bibles to clowns doing face painting.

Matt clasped Sierra's hand and they walked down the sidewalk. Though they hadn't been together all that long, they'd quickly gotten to the point where they didn't always need to talk.

Sometimes it scared him how close they'd become. And other times he felt like laughing out loud with sheer joy. It was strange how things happened, he mused. He never would have believed he would be so content with one woman. Of course, at one time, he'd wondered if he'd ever fall in love.

Matt slanted a sideways glance at Sierra. Her blond hair was drawn back from her face with a pair of gold clips and her teal cotton shirt brought out the color in her eyes. Her skirt was made of some soft fabric that clung gently to her before flaring out, exposing legs that went on forever.

His mouth went dry just thinking about the surprise he'd planned for the end of the evening. The ring was in his pocket. All he could hope was that this festival wouldn't last long. He couldn't wait to tell her how he felt.

He'd never known another woman who could make him so crazy. When he wasn't with her, he thought about her. She was on his mind 24/7. Last night, when he'd thought she'd been with another man . . .

A knot formed in the pit of his stomach, but he forced himself to relax. The attraction in this relationship wasn't one-sided. He'd seen the way she'd looked at him tonight.

"Isn't that the most beautiful thing you've ever seen?" Sierra's voice held a wistful edge.

Matt turned and followed the direction of her gaze. One of the booths was holding a raffle and the prize was displayed on a raised platform.

He tilted his head and stared at the cherry wood box with fabric on top. "What is it?"

"It's a hope chest, silly. Come with me. I

want to get a better look." Sierra smiled and tugged on his hand.

Matt followed behind her, unable to keep from smiling at her exuberance.

"You can have a chance to win for only a dollar," an old man with a raspy voice wheezed. "Looks like the young lady is quite smitten with it."

Matt gave the man a brief smile and followed Sierra to the hope chest. He tilted his head and stared at it. The box was a fine piece of workmanship, he'd give it that. "What's it for?"

"Hope chests go way back," Sierra said. "Brides-to-be used them to store the linens and household goods they would use after they married."

Matt nodded. "A storage chest."

"In a way," Sierra said. "But they're more than that. My mother used to say hope chests were a place where you placed your hopes and dreams. And when you married, your husband would make them come true."

From what his father had told him about Stella Carlyle, Matt was having trouble reconciling a woman who divorced her last husband after only five months to the romantic Sierra was describing.

"Do you have a hope chest?" Matt asked Sierra.

Sierra laughed and shook her head. "I don't believe that anyone can make my dreams come true. That is strictly up to me."

Though normally Matt would have solidly endorsed such an attitude, he found himself wanting to argue with her, to tell her that whatever her dreams, *he* would make them come true.

"Still, it is beautiful." Her gaze rested admiringly on the gleaming cherry wood even as her fingers caressed the finish.

"Why don't you buy a ticket?" Matt urged. "Maybe you'll win."

Sierra chuckled. "I'm not that lucky," she said with a self-deprecating smile. "Besides hope chests are for dreamers, for women who still believe happily-ever-after is possible."

Her smile faded and she turned away from the chest.

Anger rose inside Matt at the man who'd hurt her so badly. Still, though Sierra might say she'd lost faith in happily-ever-after, Matt's instincts told him she still wanted to believe.

He placed an arm around her shoulder and gave it a little squeeze. "I see only good things in your future."

Sierra laughed. "And just what makes

you such an expert?"

"I'm psychic," Matt said in a loud tone and Sierra promptly shushed him.

"This is a Christian Praise Festival," Sierra reminded him. "No psychics allowed."

"That's too bad," Matt murmured. "Because I'd just had a vision about what was going to happen when we return to my place. And, it's really good."

A spark of interest flared in her green eyes. "Tell me."

"Can't." Matt shook his head, keeping his face serious. "This is a Christian Praise Festival, remember? No psychics allowed."

"I won't tell anyone," she teased.

"Nope," he said. "You have to wait until later."

Sierra's smile dimmed.

Of course, there wasn't one ounce of psychic ability flowing through Matt's veins. Unless, of course, you counted the sudden premonition he had that something was bothering her.

"Is anything wrong?" He snaked an arm around her waist and pulled her to him. With one finger, Matt tipped her face up to his, wishing they weren't surrounded by onlookers so he could kiss her troubles away.

"I'm fine," she said, offering him a smile

that didn't quite meet her eyes. "Just a little tired."

"I saw some cotton candy up ahead," he said. He reached into his pocket and pulled out several bills. "Why don't you go buy us some instant energy?"

She took the money from his fingers, but stared up at him with a puzzled frown. "Where are you going to be?"

Matt gestured with his head to a large group of men standing talking on the other side of the walkway. "I saw someone I know and I thought I'd pop over and say a quick hello. Won't take but a second."

"Okay." To his surprise, Sierra rose on her tiptoes and brushed a quick kiss on his cheek. "Don't be long."

"You've got a pretty wife there, mister," the old man said, watching Sierra's hips sway gently from side to side as she walked away. "Real pretty."

Matt didn't correct the man's mistaken impression. Instead he pulled out his wallet, peeled off a hundred dollar bill and handed it to the old man. "I'll take one hundred tickets."

"Your missus is going to be one happy camper if you win." The guy cackled. "I saw the way she looked at the chest."

Matt offered the man a polite smile,

filled out a form with his name and address and watched the guy count off a hundred of the tiny ticket stubs.

The way Matt figured it, Sierra deserved a man who could make her dreams come true.

And he was just the man to make that happen.

Sierra paid the woman for two bags of cotton candy and opened hers while waiting for Matt. A light breeze off the ocean caressed her and she lifted her face to the sun.

It was too nice a day to feel blue, she decided. Nothing was going to change the fact that she and Matt would soon be apart, so she might as well enjoy every moment they *were* together.

"Hope I didn't keep you waiting long," Matt said, openly eyeing the cotton candy.

"There's still some for you," Sierra said with an impish grin, plopping a big wad of the sticky substance in her mouth. "But if you would have taken much longer I couldn't guarantee anything."

His gaze moved to her lips and his gaze darkened. Sierra's heart picked up speed. She had the crazy premonition that he was going to kiss her.

Right then and there.

She took a step toward him.

"Sierra," a deep voice boomed. "We thought that was you."

Sierra shifted her gaze and gave a delighted gasp. She immediately moved from Matt's side to give each of her former high-school classmates a big hug. "Caesar. Lily. I haven't seen you two in forever. Where have you been keeping yourselves?"

"We moved to Sacramento after graduation." Lily seemed older and her dark eyes more tired than Sierra remembered. "But when Raul was born, we started saving our money to move back."

"You have a child?" For the first time Sierra noticed the stroller next to Lily. "I hadn't heard. I love babies."

Sierra crouched down and leaned close to get a good look. When she did, she swallowed a gasp. The dark-eyed baby was horribly scarred. For a moment, she just froze, afraid the surprise and revulsion she felt was written all over her face.

Matt moved closer and leaned over. Unlike her he didn't seem at all stunned. He held out his finger and the baby took it, smiling widely when he jiggled his finger up and down.

"He's got a beautiful smile," Matt said,

glancing up at the Hispanic couple. "And he's very alert."

Sierra nodded, glad for something positive to say. "Very alert."

Caesar took Lily's arm and gave it a squeeze. "Raul is smart. All the doctors say so."

"How was he burned?" Matt asked in a quiet tone.

Caesar and Lily glanced at each other and Sierra realized he was a stranger to them.

Sierra made quick work of the introductions, the question still hanging in the air.

"He was hurt at the day care," Caesar said in a halting tone. "They said it was an accident, but one of the teachers told me it was pure negligence, that it never should have happened."

Lily's eyes filled with tears. "It was big and new and we thought they'd take good care of him."

"The day care has paid for his medical expenses," Caesar said. "They've been very helpful. But now they want us to sign a paper saying they've fulfilled their obligation. The doctors say he'll need many more surgeries. . . ."

Caesar's voice broke and Lily exhaled a ragged breath and patted his arms.

"Don't sign any paper," Matt said. "Not until you have an attorney look at it."

"That's what my mother said." Lily cast a sideways glance at her husband. "The problem is we don't have money to pay a lawyer."

"There are some legal-aid clinics here in town that might be able to help," Sierra said. "I think they charge a sliding scale —"

Matt snorted and waved a dismissive hand. "They wouldn't give this case the time and attention it deserves."

"But *any* attention is better than *no* attention," Sierra pointed out. Granted, the overworked legal-aid attorneys already had full plates, but she'd known people who'd gone there and had received help. "And with no money they don't have any other options."

"They won't do the case justice," Matt insisted, his chin rising in a stubborn gesture.

Sierra could sense her friends' confusion and she hastened to explain. "Matt is an attorney. His firm is in the process of opening a Santa Barbara branch."

"You've dealt with this type of situation before?" Lily asked.

Matt nodded.

Hope flared in Caesar's eyes. "Maybe you could help us?"

Sierra knew that even if her friends worked three jobs each, they wouldn't be able to afford Matt's fees. She steeled herself for his refusal.

"I'd be glad to help." Matt reached into his pocket, pulled out his wallet and retrieved a business card. "Just call that number and tell the secretary that we'd talked and I wanted you to set up an appointment. In the meantime, don't sign anything. Refer any contacts from the day care or their attorneys to me. Understand?"

Caesar nodded and exchanged a glance with his wife. "How can we ever thank you?"

Matt smiled and gestured to the stroller. "Take good care of the little guy."

Sierra waited until Caesar and Lily were out of earshot before speaking, her brain a mass of confusion. "They're never going to be able to pay your fee."

Matt plucked his bag of cotton candy from her hands. "I'd best get to this before you eat it all."

Sierra glanced down and realized with a start, she'd not only eaten all of hers, but some of his.

"They aren't going to be able to afford you," she repeated.

Matt grinned. "Few can."

Sierra grabbed his shirtsleeve in frustration. "Be serious."

He opened the plastic bag and plopped a big bite of cotton candy into his mouth before answering. "I didn't go to law school to help Hollywood stars get off on shoplifting charges."

"You didn't?"

He laughed. "Hard as it may seem for you to believe, I like to help people. I do more than my share of pro bono work. Caesar and his wife fall into that category."

"You don't even know them."

"They're friends of yours." Matt tugged on a strand of her hair. "Besides, how many times do I have to tell you, I'm a nice guy."

"You *were* nice to Raul," she said, still trying to make sense of his behavior.

"What was I supposed to do?" he asked, sticking another glob of spun sugar into his mouth. "Kick the stroller?"

"I don't know," Sierra said. "But you told me you didn't like kids."

She didn't know what made her keep pressing the point, but she couldn't make herself stop.

"I like kids, I'm just not very good with them." Matt shrugged. "Hopefully I'll be better with my own."

"Your own?" Sierra's mouth dropped open. "I thought you didn't even want children."

"I didn't." He smiled and winked. "Until I met you."

The cotton candy was long gone and the crowds had started to thin but Matt didn't even think about asking Sierra if she was ready to leave. Sara Michaels, one of the Christian artists brought in by the Coalition of Churches, would be taking the stage in less than a half hour and Sierra had been eagerly anticipating the performance.

So, Matt tempered his impatience and found them a shady spot under a tree to the right of where an impromptu stage had been set up. Sierra unfolded the blanket they'd retrieved from the car, spread it on the ground and they settled in to wait for the show to begin.

Sitting with his back against a tree and his arm around Sierra's shoulder, Matt enjoyed the unfamiliar sensation of being totally and completely content. Conversation buzzed around them as his fingers played with her hair.

Sierra's gaze focused on the cloudless sky, a tiny smile dancing at the corners of her lips.

Matt brushed his lips against her cheek, the skin soft and smooth and as warm as the sun. "Penny for your thoughts?"

She shook her head and a hint of pink that had nothing to do with the sun colored her cheeks. "It's silly."

He nibbled on her ear and she jerked away, the pink turning to red.

"Matt, stop it," she ordered. "Someone might see you."

He lifted his hand and with one finger gently tucked a strand of hair behind her ear. "Then tell me what you were thinking."

A knowing look filled her eyes. "Do you always find a way to get your way?"

He grinned. "Usually."

"You're incorrigible."

"Enough of the compliments," Matt said. "Tell me what made you smile."

"It was God's promise to Abraham," she said quickly before his mouth had a chance to make it to her neck.

He lifted a skeptical eyebrow. "Are you making this up?"

"When I looked up at the sky, it reminded me of when I was a little girl," she said. "Only then I was looking at a night sky filled with stars."

He still didn't get the connection yet,

but he could see she was working toward an explanation, so he nodded and waited for her to continue.

"I looked up and said to my mother, or —" she paused thoughtfully "— maybe it was a friend, doesn't this remind you of God's promise to Abraham?"

Now, she'd really lost him. "God's promise to Abraham?"

She nodded. "You know, that your children shall number as many as the stars in the sky."

Once again, the picture that Matt had formed in his mind of Stella, didn't jive with the woman Sierra described.

"It had to be a friend you said that to," Matt murmured.

Sierra shrugged then smiled. "I told you it wasn't that interesting."

Matt grabbed her hand and brought it to his lips. "I find everything you say fascinating."

"You do?" Her hand trembled beneath his lips and Matt smiled in satisfaction.

"Say something," he urged. "And I guarantee I'll be mesmerized."

"You want to talk?" Her voice came out in a husky croak that stirred Matt's senses.

"I'd like to do other things," he said, nipping the soft flesh of her knuckles before pulling his lips away. "But this is a little too public and if I'm not mistaken, Sara Michaels is ready to take the stage."

Sierra shifted her gaze to the stage, to the leggy blonde standing off to the side, waiting to be introduced.

She clasped Matt's hand. "I'm so glad you came with me. You're going to love her."

He met her gaze and a strange tightness gripped his heart, the words he spoke coming from deep within. "I already do."

Chapter Fifteen

I already do.

Even as Sara Michaels took the stage and the singer's sweet voice filled the air, the words echoed in Matt's mind.

He loved Sierra and with each passing moment it was getting harder not to confess that love.

His gaze shifted to her, but she was too engrossed in the performance to notice his scrutiny. He let his gaze linger. Everything he saw he liked. Unlike many of the women he'd dated in the past, Sierra was genuine. Someone he could trust.

His arm tightened around her and she looked up at him, her eyes gleaming like emeralds.

"Isn't this so much fun?" she asked, casting a quick glance at the stage to make sure she wasn't missing anything. "I told you she was fabulous."

Despite knowing a large contingent of her congregation was nearby, Matt couldn't resist. She looked so beautiful gazing up at him with such happiness in her eyes that he had to do it. He leaned over and kissed her full on the lips.

"What was that for?" she asked when he'd finished, her breath rapid, her eyes even more glittery.

"It's because *you're* fabulous," he said. "It's because I —"

Before he could get the words out, she surprised him by flinging her arms around his neck and kissing him, the intensity of her response taking him by surprise.

"Wow," he said. "What was that for?"

She smiled and cupped his face in her hands. "Because I think you're fabulous, too."

His heart overflowed with emotion and Matt wanted nothing more than to confess his love right then and there. But then he remembered the surprise waiting for them at home and he bit back the words.

"Let's go back to my house," he said, meeting her gaze.

"Now?"

"As soon as she's through performing," Matt said in a low, husky voice taut with emotion. "There's so much I want to say to you, so much I want —"

"There's something I have to say to you, too."

The audience applauded and Sierra rose to her feet. "Let's go."

She wondered what he wanted to say to her. Though she was curious, she knew it wouldn't be nearly as important as what she had to say to him.

Sierra smoothed the skirt of her dress while Matt folded the blanket into a perfect square. She liked the way he operated, with neat precision. With Matt what you saw was what you got.

What if he hates me for lying to him? Her heart clenched.

He took her hand and met her gaze. "Ready?"

She nodded, not trusting herself to speak.

"Sierra."

Sierra turned and saw Carl striding toward her through the crowd. Matt must have seen him at the same time because his hand tightened around hers.

She wasn't surprised that when Carl drew close, Matt released her hand and looped his arm around her shoulders in a deliberately possessive gesture.

"I'm glad I found you," Carl said, his face red with exertion. "Your mother has been trying to reach you."

Sierra's heart stopped. It wasn't so much Carl's words as the look on his face. She took a step forward, her hand reaching out to touch the minister's arm, icy fingers of dread creeping up her spine. "What's wrong?"

"It's Maddie," he said. "There's been an accident."

Sierra swayed and would have fallen if Matt hadn't put a steadying arm around her waist.

"What kind of accident?"

"It seems she had a little run-in with a car," Carl said trying to joke, but failing miserably. Though she could tell he was trying to be reassuring, Sierra could see a flicker of fear in his eyes.

"But she's okay, isn't she?" Her voice was shrill and several people turned to stare, but Sierra didn't care. Her baby had to be okay. She couldn't live if something happened to Maddie.

Dear God, please help Maddie. Please take care of her. Please let her be okay.

Sierra swiped at the tears streaming down her face with the back of her hand, her entire attention focused on Carl.

"She's okay, isn't she, Carl?" Sierra repeated.

"Honey —" Matt tried to take her arm, but she pushed him away.

"Carl, tell me Maddie is okay," Sierra demanded, desperation lacing her tone.

"Of course she is," Carl said in a soothing tone. "Everyone knows Santa Barbara General has the best doctors."

"Hospital. Doctors." Black dots flashed before Sierra's eyes, but she took a deep breath and determinedly forced away the impending darkness. Later, when she was alone she would fall apart. Not now. Not when Maddie needed her.

"Let me take you to the hospital." Carl stepped closer and took Sierra's arm.

"I'll take her to the hospital," Matt said firmly and Carl paused, shifting his gaze to Sierra.

"Matt will take me." Sierra nodded convulsively and swallowed a sob. "But you'll be there, too, won't you, Carl?"

"I'll meet you there," Carl said.

"Thank you," Sierra whispered, tears flooding her eyes. "Pray for her, Carl. I don't know what I'd do if something happened. . . ."

"She'll pull through." Carl patted her arm awkwardly. "And as far as the praying, I started that the minute I heard the news."

"We need to get to the hospital," Sierra said to Matt. "I have to see Maddie. I have to know she's okay."

They hurried to Matt's car without

speaking and it wasn't until they were halfway to the hospital that Matt turned to her.

"Who is Maddie?" he asked, his voice filled with concern. "I don't think I've ever heard you speak of her."

Sierra leaned back in her seat, the image of her daughter's blond pigtails and infectious smile flashing before her, tearing at her heartstrings.

Dear God, please take care of my baby. She's . . .

"Sierra?" Matt's words broke into her supplication. "Who is Maddie?"

Dabbing at her tears with an already soaked paper napkin, Sierra lifted her eyes to his. "She's my daughter."

Matt had only been punched in the stomach once in his life. He'd been ten and he and his friend, Kevin Blanchard, had been goofing around. The air had shot from his lungs and his stomach had hurt like hell. He felt the same way now. "Daughter?"

Sierra nodded. "She's four. And she's the sweetest, most wonderful . . ."

Her voice broke and she turned her head toward the window as if embarrassed by her tears.

A daughter? She has a child? The knowledge that she'd deliberately hidden that fact stabbed him like a knife. He wanted to ask what else hadn't she told him?

But there was a time and place for everything and this definitely wasn't the time for twenty questions. He couldn't, wouldn't, add to her stress. There would be time enough for answers later.

She didn't have to tell him to go fast, his foot stomped heavily on the pedal and if there was even the slightest chance of making a light, he made it. They arrived at the hospital in record time.

The moment he pulled into the parking lot and stopped the car, Sierra was out the door and headed toward the front entrance. Matt had to run to keep up.

"I'm looking for Maddie Summers," Sierra said to the clerk at the information desk. "She's my daughter and she was hit by a car."

The white-haired woman punched the name into the computer and the eyes behind the bifocals were kind when they rose to meet Sierra's gaze. "She's still in the emergency room. It's down the hall —"

"I know where it is." Sierra tossed the words over her shoulder as she raced down the hall.

Matt followed behind.

A trim stylish woman about fifty paced in front of the nurses' station. Her eyes were red and puffy and what lipstick she may have put on, had long ago been chewed off.

"Where is she?" Sierra demanded, rushing up to the woman.

"In X ray," the woman said, taking Sierra's arm. "They think she might have a slight concussion."

Sierra's mouth opened and her hand rose to her mouth.

"She was unconscious when the paramedics brought her in," the woman said in a reassuring tone, blinking back her own tears. "But she's conscious now and I told her you'd be here soon."

"So she knew you?" Sierra asked. "She talked to you?"

The woman nodded. "She wanted to know if we could go for ice cream."

Sierra closed her eyes and lifted her face. "Thank you, Lord."

"Praise to God, indeed," the woman echoed. "It was a miracle she wasn't hurt more seriously."

"What happened?"

"She was playing out in the drive with her ball and it rolled into the street." The woman's face blanched just remembering. "She went after it. I called for her to stop, but she didn't listen. When the car came . . ."

The woman shuddered and tears slipped down her cheeks.

"Mother, it's not your fault." Sierra wrapped her arms around the woman and pulled her close. "Not at all."

Matt could only stare, wondering when he'd slipped into the twilight zone. First Sierra says she has a child, now she's calling this woman, Mother? How could that be? Stella Carlyle was a blue-eyed blonde and this brunette had brown eyes.

The two women clung to each other for several heartbeats before separating, each of them sniffling.

"I knew you'd gone to the Praise Festival but I didn't know how to get a hold of you," the woman explained. "Then I saw Carl in the hall — he was here seeing a parishioner — and he said he'd find you."

"He did," Sierra said.

"Where is he?" The woman looked around, her gaze brushing right over Matt. "Didn't he bring you?"

Sierra shook her head. "Matt brought me."

Her mother's puzzled gaze settled on him. "Matt?"

Sierra's gaze shifted to him and it was as if she could sense his confusion. Her lips curved up in a sad smile.

"Matt, this is my mother, Peggy Summers," she said. "Mother, this is my friend, Matt Dixon."

"Dixon?" Peggy paused. "Any relation to Lawrence Dixon?"

Matt nodded. "He's my father. Do you know him?"

Normally, when someone found out he was Dix's son, they were excited. After all, Dix was a celebrity of sorts in the region. If they didn't know him personally, they'd read of his exploits in the paper or seen him interviewed on the six o'clock news.

But Peggy didn't seem excited, or even pleased. She cast her daughter a disapproving look. "*This* is the man you've been seeing? What is wrong with you?"

"Mother, Matt is nothing like his father," Sierra said. "He —"

"You know my father?" Matt interrupted, casting Sierra a questioning look.

"She should," Peggy interjected. "He represented her ex-husband in the divorce. Jerry should be in prison now, instead of walking the streets with law-abiding citizens. But your father —"

"Mother, that's quite enough," Sierra said sharply. "Not another word."

Peggy shut her mouth, took a deep breath and shot Matt an apologetic look. "I'm sorry. The sins of the father don't fall on the son. I know that."

The woman wiped a trembling hand across her face. "This has just been the most trying day. Please forgive my rudeness."

"I understand," Matt said, though he didn't understand at all.

When this was over, he and Sierra would have to sit down and have a long talk. And he would get to the bottom of what was really going on.

Chapter Sixteen

It was after nine by the time Sierra got Maddie back to their apartment and into bed. The CT scan had shown only a slight concussion and although she had lots of bumps and bruises, miraculously nothing was broken.

Sierra had been able to take her daughter home from the hospital, with strict instructions on symptoms to watch for in the next few days. Her mother had wanted to spend the night, but Sierra had sent her home, knowing if she stayed her mother would spend the night sitting at her granddaughter's bedside, watching the little girl sleep.

Instead, Sierra thought, I'll get to be the one watching her sleep and sending prayers of thanks heavenward. She leaned over and brushed a light kiss against the purple bruise on her daughter's forehead.

Thank you, God.

Matt had left the hospital shortly after Carl had arrived, pronouncing her "in good hands."

Matt had been polite, but distant, patting her on the shoulder when he'd said goodbye. She'd seen the hurt and confusion in his eyes. At the time there had been nothing she could do but let him go. Maddie was her focus, her priority and there'd been no time to give him the explanations he deserved.

But there was time now, and it wasn't going to get any easier the longer she waited. She lifted the cordless from its base and, before she lost her nerve, quickly dialed his number.

He answered on the first ring.

"Matt," she said. "It's me."

"How's your daughter?" he asked, his tone one commonly reserved for strangers or casual acquaintances.

"Just a mild concussion and some bumps and bruises," she said. "They let her come home."

"I'm glad," he said. "I could see how worried you were."

Some of the warmth had returned to his voice and hope rose inside her.

"There's so much I need to tell you," she said. "So much I need to explain."

"Yes, you do," he agreed.

The coolness was back in his voice and the burgeoning hope faded.

"I'd rather explain in person," she said.

"And, I'd rather do it sooner than later. Could you come over?"

She held her breath, unsure of his reaction. At least he'd answered her call and had been civil. If she were in his place, she'd be livid.

"I can come over, but I don't think I know where you live," he said finally. "I'm guessing it's not the house on Arrellaga."

"No, it's not," Sierra said. "It's the apartment you were at the other night. Don't ring the bell. Just knock lightly and I'll open the door."

"I'll be there in a half hour," he said.

"Matt," she said quickly before he hung up. "I'm sorry I lied to you."

He paused for a long moment. "I'm sorry you did, too."

To quell her nervousness, Sierra picked up the house while waiting for Matt to arrive. Because she'd always insisted that Maddie put away her toys after playing with them, the place wasn't really messy. But she put the newspaper into the magazine rack, plumped up some pillows on the sofa and ran a dust rag across any bare surfaces. Then she put some tea on to brew.

The tea kettle had just started to whistle when she heard a light tapping at the door. She shut off the gas and transferred the tea kettle to another burner before moving to the door.

Her heart pounded in her chest and when she saw the grim look on his face through the peephole, whatever hope she'd had vanished.

With trembling hands, Sierra flipped the dead bolt, released the chain and opened the door.

"Come in." She gestured him inside with one hand. "I just finished making some tea. Would you like some?"

He met her gaze, his blue eyes unflinching. "The only thing I want is answers."

Apprehension skittered through her. Why had she ever agreed when Libby had proposed this crazy scheme? How could she have ever thought it would be fun?

"Have a seat," Sierra said. "I'll be glad to answer whatever questions you have."

A half hour later, the lines between his eyebrows had deepened and if anything, he was even more cool and distant than he'd been when he'd walked through the door.

"Let me summarize." He leaned forward and spread his fingers on the coffee table that stood between them. "In essence everything you told me was a lie. Everything that existed between us was a lie."

"Not everything," Sierra said, resisting the urge to reach out and comfort him and in turn, comfort herself. "I —"

"You lied about who you are, where you live, what you do," he said, without giving her a chance to continue. "I realize now that I fell in love with someone who doesn't exist."

"You love me?" Sierra's heart quickened. She extended her hand to him but he sat back, putting himself out of reach.

"Not you," he said, the sad glint in his eyes softening the harshness of his tone. "The woman I thought you were."

"But I am —"

He waved aside her protests. "I can't tell you how many divorces I've done where the guy has told me he never really knew his wife. I'd always think, how could you *not* know her? You fell in love with the woman. You married her. Now, for the first time I understand how that could happen."

"I've already explained," Sierra said, sensing him slipping away but powerless to stop him. "Libby and I switched places just for fun. It was just a game. No one was supposed to get hurt."

"A game?"

The condemnation she heard in his voice hit a nerve. She may have been the one most at fault, but he certainly wasn't blameless.

"Don't even try to tell me you weren't playing your own little game," Sierra said. "You weren't looking for anything permanent, you told me that yourself. You wanted a summer romance, no strings attached. So what difference did it make that I was divorced with a child? I know what you wanted. You wanted me temporarily, not permanently in your life."

He stared at her for a long moment. "You don't know anything."

Tears filled Sierra's eyes and she angrily swiped at them with the back of her hand.

Matt rose from the chair, his face expressionless. "I need to be going."

"Tell me you don't hate me," she said, rising to her feet, a touch of hysteria underlying her words. She could bear the thought of him not loving her, but not the thought of him hating her.

"I don't hate you," he said softly, his hand closing over hers.

When his warm flesh touched hers, it took all Sierra's inner strength not to give in to a crazy urge to pull him close and beg him to stay.

Instead, she walked with him to the door in silence.

"Like you said, it's probably good it ended now," he said.

Though Sierra didn't recall ever making that statement, she nodded her agreement.

She closed the door behind him. And not until she heard his footsteps head down the stairs did Sierra allow her heart to break.

Chapter Seventeen

It had been nine days, ten hours and fifteen minutes since Matt had last seen Sierra. And he missed her desperately. He still couldn't believe it had all been part of some offbeat game. A game devised for adults, not children.

Children.

Matt leaned back in his office chair and raked his fingers through his hair. Sierra had a daughter. That's what had really thrown him for a loop. The other stuff he might be able to forgive, but forgetting to mention you had a child was big.

He'd never wanted to be a stepparent. Never. From what he'd observed in the divorce cases he'd handled, raising children that weren't your own was a thankless task and a constant bone of contention in a marriage.

That's why he hadn't called Sierra. She loved her daughter and Matt knew they were a package deal.

"Mr. Dixon?" Rachel Easton, the new office receptionist, stuck her head inside the door. "Your mother is here and wants to speak with you. Are you available?"

Matt leaned back in his chair and nodded. "Send her in."

One of the good things that had come out of his association with Sierra was his newfound relationship with his mother. After he and Sierra had parted, Matt had found himself with lots of time to think. And, Sierra's words about forgiveness wouldn't let go.

Finally, he'd pushed aside what remaining hurt and anger still lingered in his heart and called his mother back. They'd met several times in the past week and though the relationship was still somewhat strained, it was definitely on the mend.

"I hope I'm not intruding," Janice Dixon waltzed into the room, a shopping bag in each hand. She was tall and stylishly slender, just like Tori, and remarkably attractive for someone in her early fifties. Her hair was cut in a short bob with highlights hiding whatever gray lurked in the blond strands. She reminded Matt more of a fashion consultant than a mother.

He rose to his feet and rounded the desk to greet her. "Of course you're not intruding. Let me take those bags. Have a seat. I'll have Rachel bring in some iced tea."

"Sounds fabulous." Janice handed Matt her bags and elegantly lowered herself into one of the two tall wing chairs that faced the desk. "They say it's only seventy-eight outside, but it seems hotter than that to me."

Matt placed the bags to the side and buzzed Rachel. In only moments, the pretty brunette appeared with two tall glasses.

Taking a seat in the second chair, Matt took a sip of his tea and waited for his mother to tell him the reason for her visit. Though he had no doubt she'd been in the neighborhood, he'd discovered that Janice Dixon was a planner. That meant this wasn't any spur-of-the-moment visit. For whatever reason, she'd made a special point to stop by today.

She took a dainty sip of tea, then placed it on the desk. "I talked to your father last night. We had a nice conversation."

Matt didn't know what surprised him most, that she'd talked to his father or that she could label any conversation between the two of them "nice."

"You look surprised," she observed.

"I am," Matt said honestly. "I didn't think you'd contact him."

She lifted a perfectly tweezed eyebrow.

"There were things I had to say. Things he had to hear."

Matt had heard the entire story of how she'd felt trapped and unhappy in her life as wife and mother. How she had a chance for a great job in Hong Kong but she knew Dix would never let the children leave the country with her. How she'd felt she had no choice but to leave them behind.

Matt had accepted her explanation because it was fact. But he couldn't help but think about Sierra and how she would have handled the situation. He couldn't imagine Sierra leaving a child of hers behind, no matter what the reason. Of course, knowing how she felt about the sanctity of marriage, he couldn't imagine her ever getting divorced, either.

"Things to say?" Matt ventured when she didn't immediately continue.

"I wanted him to know that while it wasn't that hard for me to make the decision to leave, it *was* hard for me to stay away."

Matt shifted in his chair. This was something new, something she hadn't mentioned in their previous meetings. "Why did you then? Stay away, I mean."

The smile that seemed to be perpetually on her lips dimmed. "Foolish pride. The feeling that I'd made my bed and I had to lie in it."

"You *wanted* to come back but you let your pride stand in the way?" Matt's voice rose despite his best efforts to control it. He didn't want to judge her, that would be pointless, but he remembered all too well the loneliness that had been such a part of him all those years after she'd left.

"It's harder than you realize." His mother's blue eyes flashed. "I wanted to call but I kept putting it off. It's not easy to admit you've made a mistake and ask for forgiveness. Then, the weeks turned into months and the months into years and I figured it would be easier on all of us if I stayed away."

"Well, it wasn't easier on me," Matt said, meeting her gaze, feeling the anger rise unbidden inside him. "Or on Tori. So the only one it was easier on had to be you."

"I paid for it." A flush swept across his mother's cheeks. "Every birthday, every holiday, I wondered what it would have been like if I'd just made the call, if I'd just gotten on that plane, if I'd just . . ."

Her voice trailed off for a moment before she took a deep breath and lifted her chin. "But I didn't. And I've learned that we have to live with the choices we've made, right or wrong."

"What would you do differently now?" Matt asked, though it scarcely mattered. "If you could do it over?"

A sad smile flitted across his mother's lips. "If I had it to do over, I never would have left in the first place."

Sierra stared down at her chocolate-and-marshmallow sundae and sighed. "Don't even tell me that you're not going to eat that," Libby said. "That's your favorite kind."

"I don't have much of an appetite." Sierra lifted her spoon and dipped it into the mound of whipped cream topping the sundae.

"Maddie's doing okay, isn't she?" Libby's eyebrows pulled together. "There's nothing going on that you haven't told me?"

A smile lifted Sierra's lips. "Good as new. Mom and I took her to the doctor yesterday and he released her from his care."

"I'm so glad." Libby reached over and gave Sierra's hand a squeeze. "You know I love the little munchkin."

"I know you do." Sierra topped Libby's hand with her own. "You've been such a good friend to me."

"I *am* a good friend," Libby said, tossing her head. "Maybe even the best friend one could ever have."

Sierra laughed and Libby's lips curved up in satisfaction.

"It's good to see you laugh again," Libby said. "That split with Matt has had you down in the dumps."

"I miss him," Sierra said simply. It was an understatement of massive proportions. Every fiber of her being longed to see him, to talk to him, to hold him close. He filled her thoughts during the day and haunted her dreams at night.

"You still haven't heard from him?" Libby took a sip of her strawberry soda and her eyes widened.

"Not one peep," Sierra said with a sigh. "Not that I really expected to anyway. We've said everything there was to say. What's left?"

"I still don't understand what the big deal was. So you're not me. He didn't fall in love with me —"

"He didn't fall in love with me, either, Libby," Sierra interrupted. "Or at least if he did, he never told me about it."

"Okay." Libby waved a dismissive hand at the mettlesome detail. "He grew fond of you, then. Would that be a fair statement?"

Sierra nodded. Matt cared for her. That much at least she knew was true.

"So, what did it matter if your name was Sierra Summers or Libby Carlyle?" Libby asked. "Or if you had tons of money or —"

"No money." Sierra filled in the blank.

"Exactly," Libby said. "You're still the same person."

"Except," Sierra said. "I'm divorced. And I have a daughter."

Libby's gaze narrowed. "You think this is all about the munchkin? He doesn't want her?"

"He doesn't even know her," Sierra said. "But he's never wanted to raise someone else's kids. He said that to me before."

"But anyone who knows Maddie loves her," Libby said.

"That's true," Sierra said. "But Matt doesn't know Maddie and he's not going to give himself the chance to get to know her."

"Then you're better off without him."

"I agree totally," Sierra said.

But she couldn't help but wonder if keeping her distance from Matt was the right thing to do, why did it feel so wrong?

Libby held Maddie's hand tight in hers as they crossed State Street. "Aunt Libby has to stop by and pick up some important papers on the way to the store. Okay?"

Maddie looked up from the double-dip cone that Libby had just bought her at the Creamery and nodded, her little mouth closing around the top of the cone.

Libby cringed at the sight of the strawberry ice cream already dripping down the sides. She wished she would have thought to grab a few napkins. She quickened her steps and prayed Matt had some in his office.

The door dinged as she opened it and Libby swept past the receptionist without stopping. "Mr. Dixon is expecting us."

Matt was on the phone when she entered the office and a frown crossed his face when he caught sight of a small child at her side.

A sense of unease coursed through Libby and she wondered if she'd made a mistake. It had seemed like such a clever notion. In fact, in the peacefulness of her home, the idea had seemed positively brilliant.

Just like she'd told Sierra, everyone who knew Maddie loved her. So, all she needed to do was to introduce Matt to Maddie and he'd love her. Then, there wouldn't be anything standing between Sierra and

Matt but pride and if she had to, Libby knew she could figure a way around that, too.

"I hope you don't mind," Libby said, "that I brought Maddie with me. Sierra is in class and I'm baby-sitting."

Maddie looked up, her lips covered with strawberry ice cream. "I'm not a baby."

"Of course you're not, sweetheart."

By now the ice cream was running down the cone and onto Maddie's hand. In a few moments it would be on Matt's thick plush carpet.

For a second, Libby wished Sierra were there. Her friend always seemed prepared for these types of catastrophes.

Matt pushed the buzzer. "Rachel, could you bring in some napkins, please? Right away."

In only seconds, the napkins were in Libby's hands, but it would take more than paper to remove the stickiness from Maddie's hands and face.

"There's a sink just through there," Matt said, pointing down a short hall. "She needs her hands and face washed."

Libby stared at Maddie for a long moment as if the thought had never occurred to her. "I believe you're right. Why don't you clean her up while I look through these papers on the Advocacy Center?"

Matt's mouth dropped open.

"I can do it, Mr. Dixon," Rachel said, and Libby suddenly realized the woman had never left the room.

"Thank you —" Matt began.

"I'm afraid not." Libby shot the woman a polite, but firm smile. "I don't know you and I don't let Maddie go with anyone I don't know. Mr. Dixon will have to take her."

"Why don't *you* take her?" Matt said to Libby. "And then, when you get back, you can sign the papers."

Libby made a great show of glancing at her watch. "I'm afraid I don't have time to do both. And you did say the papers had to be signed today?"

Matt stifled a groan. The Advocacy Center was heading into the homestretch and the cost had run over early projections. Stella had agreed to kick in the extra and that was the reason for Libby's visit today.

"I'd like to review this document before I write the check," Libby said. "I guess I could come back another time. . . ."

"No, you sit right there and read," Matt said, glancing down at the little girl. "I can take her."

He gestured with his head down the hall. "Come on, honey. Let's get your hands washed."

But the child didn't take a step. Instead, she moved closer to Libby, her blue eyes wide and large.

"It's okay, princess." Libby crouched down beside the little girl and shot her a reassuring smile. "Mr. Dixon is a friend of mine. And he's your mommy's friend and Reverend Carl's friend. He won't hurt you."

The tightness in the little girl's face eased and she held out her hand to Matt.

Though it was sticky, Matt took it without flinching. He couldn't help but wonder why Libby felt it necessary to reassure the child that he wouldn't hurt her?

Since she hadn't really spoken much, Matt expected that they'd walk to the rest room in silence, he'd wash her hands and face and they'd return to his office. Easy enough.

But Libby's reassurance must have worked because they'd barely taken two steps when Maddie started talking.

"My mommy is at school," she said. "That's why I'm with Aunt Libby. Next year I'm going to school, too."

"Is that right?" Matt asked.

"Mmm, hmm," Maddie said. "I'm going to be five next year."

"Getting old," was the only thing Matt could think to say.

He discovered she really didn't need much encouragement to continue talking. In the short distance to the washroom, Matt heard about her mother's new job, her grandmother's cookies and a doll that had recently lost its head.

She was a cute little girl, he decided. Her blond hair, pulled back in a long ponytail and tied with a ribbon, was several shades lighter than her mother's and though her eyes were blue, not green, she reminded him of Sierra.

"Aunt Libby got me a double-dip cone," Maddie announced.

"That's a lot of ice cream for a little girl to eat," Matt said.

"I could have eaten it all," she said, her blue eyes serious. "But it melted."

She gazed down at her once-clean white top then lifted her eyes to him. "Mommy's going to be mad."

Matt couldn't imagine Sierra being angry over something as inconsequential as ice cream on a shirt. She seemed, he thought, like a mother who wouldn't sweat the small stuff, but who wouldn't be a pushover, either.

And she'd never leave her child.

"You've got a nice mommy," he said, opening the door to the washroom and ushering her inside.

"You know my mommy?" Maddie stood still while he wetted a paper towel and carefully wiped the stickiness from her face.

"I've met her," Matt said, getting another paper towel for her hands.

"My mommy's the prettiest mommy in the whole world," Maddie announced. "Rev'nd Carl says so."

Matt's hand tightened around the paper towel and a knot formed in the pit of his stomach. Now that he was out of the picture, it didn't surprise him that the good pastor wasn't wasting any time making his move. "Does Reverend Carl come over to your apartment?"

Maddie nodded vigorously. "I like him. He plays Candy Land with me."

Matt wasn't sure what Candy Land was, but he didn't ask. Interrogating a child just didn't seem right.

He finished wiping her hands. "All done."

"You're a nice man." Maddie stared at him without moving. "I like you."

Matt smiled, surprisingly touched by the

comment. "I like you, too."

Libby was waiting with the documents in hand when they strolled back into the office. She eyed Maddie with a sharp, assessing gaze and nodded her approval before turning her attention back to Matt. "We'd better get going."

"Are you going to be able to make the meeting Tuesday?" Matt asked. "I need to go over the final set of figures with you."

"Tuesday?" Libby raised a questioning eyebrow. "Who's all going to be at this meeting?"

"Just you and I," Matt said. "You could stop by the office?"

Libby smiled. "Wouldn't miss it for the world."

Chapter Eighteen

"Why don't you just call him?" Libby urged, leaning forward in her chair and almost spilling her glass of lemonade in the process.

Sierra shook her head. "It's been over two weeks. If Matt wanted to see me or speak with me, he'd have called by now."

"Maybe he's scared," Libby said. "Maybe he doesn't know what to say. Maybe he —"

"Just doesn't care," Sierra finished the sentence, the thought sending a stab of pain straight through her heart.

The evening was mild and only the merest breeze stirred the air. Sierra enjoyed sitting on Libby's veranda and chatting, as long as it wasn't about Matt.

Despite her matter-of-fact words, being without Matt hurt. She missed him with an intensity that took her breath away. But it was over. She had to accept that fact. If she'd had any doubts, the phone's silence had convinced her.

Though the last thing she wanted was to play the dating game, Carl had been coming around more often since Matt was out of the picture and she hadn't the heart to send him away.

"Did I tell you Carl is taking me to lunch next week for my birthday?" Sierra tossed off the words as if they were of no consequence.

"You're not going, are you?" Libby demanded. "Because you know if you do, he'll get the wrong idea."

"And what wrong idea would that be?"

"That you're interested in him as a man, rather than just a friend."

"Maybe I am."

"What are you saying?"

"I've been thinking," Sierra said slowly. "That maybe I should take my mother's advice and encourage Carl. If you think about it, he is perfect for me."

Carl was comfortable and predictable. He always called before he stopped over. And when he came, he never overstayed his welcome. So far, he hadn't even tried to kiss her, although last night he *had* held her hand.

And it was like holding hands with a brother. Sierra immediately shoved aside the thought.

"He is not perfect for you," Libby said. "You don't love him."

"Love is overrated." And, it hurts, Sierra added silently.

"Since when is it overrated?"

"Since forever. It just took me a while to figure it out."

"Well you're not going out with him on your birthday," Libby said. "You and I always go to lunch that day."

"Last year was the first time," Sierra said. "That hardly qualifies as always."

"It was the start of a new tradition," Libby said. "You're just going to have to call Carl and tell him you can't go."

" 'Fraid not," Sierra said. "I already said yes and he's made the reservations at Crane River."

Libby shook her head. "I can't believe you're choosing Cootie Carl over me."

"Libby," Sierra said in a low warning tone.

"Okay, okay." Libby heaved a melodramatic sigh and waved a dismissive hand. "It's your birthday. Do as you want."

"I appreciate your understanding," Sierra said with a wry smile.

"Any time." Libby heaved another sigh. "By the way, I'll be confiscating Maddie on Tuesday."

"And why would that be?" Sierra asked. Though her friend loved Maddie dearly,

Libby had never been particularly fond of watching the little girl. And this would be the second time in a week she'd asked to baby-sit.

"Birthday shopping," Libby said with a mysterious air. "And even if you put ice picks under my fingernails, I won't say more."

Sierra shook her head and laughed. Her friend was definitely up to something, but it looked as if she was going to have to wait until her birthday to find out what.

Matt breathed a sigh of relief when Libby finished reading the last of the documents and signed her name with a flourish at the bottom.

When she'd arrived at his office with Maddie in tow, he'd been unable to hide his surprise. But Libby had quickly explained Maddie's presence by saying that the two of them planned to do some birthday shopping for Sierra.

He'd expected the little girl to start chattering away as she had the other day, but instead she'd smiled shyly and settled down at his desk with a handful of crayons and a coloring book that Libby had brought with her.

Libby's cell phone rang just as she

handed Matt the last document. She answered her phone and her eyebrows immediately pulled together. "I'll be right there."

She stood. "I have to go. Carson has a crisis."

Matt nodded and rose to his feet. "We're all through here anyway."

"You don't mind, do you?" she asked. "I won't be long. While I'm gone, maybe you two could think of a gift Maddie could give her mother."

Matt realized he must have missed part of the conversation but before he could clarify, Libby was already at the door.

"Hey, aren't you forgetting something?" He cast a pointed glance at Maddie, who still sat at the desk, her head bent over the coloring book.

Libby rolled her eyes. "Weren't you listening? I said you'll have to watch Maddie for me. I won't be long. I promise."

Panic rose inside Matt. He didn't know the first thing about taking care of a four-year-old. "Libby, I can't —"

But she was gone, out the door before he could even finish the sentence.

Matt raked his fingers through his hair and shifted his gaze back to Maddie. The little girl looked up, her eyes wide and innocent. "Do you want to color with me? I'll give you the red."

Matt glanced at the stack of work on his desk and then at his watch. He didn't have time for coloring or for baby-sitting. His meeting with James Hanna was in fifteen minutes. If he left now, he'd still be able to make it.

Rachel should be able to handle Maddie. After all, hadn't she told him she had two younger sisters?

But Maddie doesn't know her. She might be scared.

The thought grabbed him and wouldn't let go. Heaving a resigned sigh, Matt hit the intercom.

"Rachel, I need you to call Mr. Hanna and reschedule our meeting."

His afternoon now free, Matt pulled a chair up to the desk and sat down next to Maddie. "Can I have a blue crayon, too?"

Maddie thought for a moment then shook her head. "Just red."

After about ten minutes, she not only let him have the blue, but the green, as well. Still, Matt hadn't really missed the other colors and he thought his red elephant looked quite nice.

A knock sounded at the door and Rachel popped her head inside. "Mr. Dixon, there's a delivery for you. It's . . . it's quite large. Too big for the outer office."

Matt paused in the middle of coloring a red moon. "Have it brought in here then."

Setting down his crayon, Matt smiled at Maddie. "I wonder what it is?"

Maddie scrambled up from the chair, her eyes dancing with excitement. "A surprise?"

A man dressed in coveralls expertly wheeled a dolly through the door and deposited the cherry wood box on the floor.

"What's this?" Matt asked.

"Didn't they notify you?" The man handed Matt a delivery confirmation form. "You won the raffle."

The man was out the door and on his way before Matt had a chance to blink.

"It's boo-ti-ful," Maddie crooned, her gaze openly admiring. "Pretty flowers."

Matt glanced down, noticing for the first time that there were indeed tiny spring flowers sewn into the tapestry on the top of the chest.

Rachel wandered into the room and stared at the cherry wood box. "What is it?"

"It's a hope chest," Matt explained, much as Sierra had to him. "Women fill them with their hopes and dreams and their husbands make those dreams come true."

"Sounds corny to me," Rachel said with a laugh.

"I like it," Maddie said, a stubborn tilt to her jaw.

"I like it too, princess." Matt gave the girl an affectionate pat on the head.

"See." Maddie glared at Rachel and her chin jutted out even farther. "*We* think it's pretty."

Rachel glanced helplessly at Matt. "I didn't say it wasn't pretty. Or that I didn't like it."

"I know you didn't," he said, in a reassuring tone.

Still, Matt couldn't help but glance down at the little girl at his side and smile. The little spitfire was so much like her mother he couldn't help but love her.

His heart skipped a beat at the realization. He'd as much as told Sierra he couldn't love a child who wasn't his, but in a matter of hours Maddie had made a mockery of his words. Without him knowing quite how, she'd stolen her way into his heart.

Loving Sierra carried with it great responsibilities, he realized. If he married Sierra, he would not only be responsible for making *her* dreams come true, but those of this little girl, as well. It was a daunting task and would likely be more than most men could handle.

But then, Matt reminded himself with a smile, he'd never been like most men.

Libby barely blinked an eye when Rachel informed her that Mr. Dixon was "in conference" with his father and didn't want to be disturbed.

Instead, she rounded Rachel's desk, rapped lightly on Matt's office door and entered the room without waiting for an acknowledgement.

Maddie was at the desk contentedly cutting out pictures from a magazine while Matt and his father sat in the two matching wing chairs.

They stopped talking when she entered and rose to their feet.

"Did you get the crisis resolved?" Matt asked. A tiny smile hovered at the corners of his lips and a knowing look filled his gaze.

"Crisis?" Libby stammered, finding it impossible to concentrate with Lawrence Dixon's steely gray eyes fixed on her. Even dressed casually in navy pants and a polo shirt, the man cut an imposing figure.

"At the restaurant?" Matt reminded her.

Libby waved one hand in the air and tried to collect her thoughts. "It was ridiculous," she said. "A complete waste of my time. How did you and Maddie get along?"

"Fine," Matt said, casting a quick glance at Maddie. "We got along just fine."

"Is this Stella's daughter?" Dix demanded.

Matt quickly introduced the two. It didn't surprise him that his father would interrupt. Dix never had liked being on the sidelines.

Dix's gaze swept approvingly over Libby. "You're a beauty, just like your mother."

Libby smiled. "Thank you."

"Your mother and I were hoping you and Matt would get together." Dix shrugged. "But I guess some things aren't meant to be."

Light dawned in Libby's eyes. "Is that what her donation to the Advocacy Center was all about? Matchmaking?"

Dix chuckled. "You know Stella. Once she gets a notion she goes full speed ahead and money is no object. For a while I thought it was actually working. Until I found out that the woman my son fell in love with was someone who was only masquerading as you."

"Fell in love?" Libby's gaze shot to Matt. "You love Sierra?"

Matt nodded. "I do."

"Why haven't you told her?" Libby demanded.

"There were some things I had to work out." Matt's gaze lingered on Maddie.

"Maddie is a wonderful girl," Libby said, her tone daring him to say anything different.

"Yes, she is," Matt concurred. "And after what she's been through, she deserves to have a father who loves her."

Understanding flickered in the depths of Libby's blue eyes. "You know about Jerry."

"Dad was telling me about the case," Matt said. "I'm surprised Sierra wanted anything to do with me, knowing my father defended the man."

"Everyone is entitled to a defense," Dix protested.

Matt shot his father a silencing glance. "Personally I agree with Sierra's mother. The man should have been locked up for what he did."

Matt's stomach churned at the thought of anyone hurting such a sweet, innocent child. He could see why Sierra found it impossible to forgive the guy. And certainly why she'd divorced him.

Libby stared at Matt for a long moment.

"Sierra's birthday is Tuesday," she said. "She's having lunch with Carl at Crane

River. He wants to be the man in her life. You can't let that happen."

"You don't like Carl?" Matt couldn't hide his surprise. He'd thought everyone liked the minister. Even Rachel had raved about Carl after hearing him preach last Sunday.

"Sierra deserves to be with someone she loves," Libby said. "And someone who loves her."

"And you think that someone is me?"

Libby tilted her head and gazed up at him through lowered lashes. "Time will tell."

The hostess at Crane River had no problem changing Carl's reservation from two people to four and seating Rachel and Matt at the table to wait for their luncheon companions.

"Are you sure they won't mind if we join them?" Rachel asked, a hint of unease in her tone.

"Not at all," Matt said. "Carl will be happy to meet an adoring parishioner."

Rachel blushed. "He's a wonderful preacher."

"And you think he's cute," Matt reminded her of what she'd told him earlier.

The pink in her cheeks turned rosy. "I

hope you're not going to tell him *that*."

Matt winked and sipped his iced tea. "Nope. I'm going to leave that for you to do."

The hostess stopped next to the table and Sierra's breath caught in her throat. She turned an accusing gaze on Carl. "What's going on here?"

"I don't have a clue." Carl's gaze shifted to Matt and his companion then back to the hostess. "Our reservations were for two."

His voice was strained and Sierra realized he'd had no part putting this chink in their plans.

Matt rose to his feet and smiled, directing his words to Carl. "I hope you don't mind if we join you. This is Rachel Eaton, my new receptionist. She's recently moved to Santa Barbara and joined your congregation. She's been dying to meet you."

"Mr. Dixon, please." The woman blushed.

Matt finished the introductions and Carl glanced at Sierra, leaving it up to her whether they joined the twosome or left.

Sierra's gaze shifted to Matt. The uncertainty in his eyes told her he was nowhere near as confident as he appeared. But it was the bald hope she glimpsed beneath the uncertainty that solidified her decision.

"I'd like some mango iced tea," she told the waitress who hovered nearby.

Surprisingly the conversation flowed easily, especially between Rachel and Carl. It turned out Rachel's father was a minister who now taught at the same seminary Carl had attended.

Sierra didn't say much. She couldn't. Every time she looked at Matt, a hard lump filled her throat. He looked so handsome in his khaki pants and a button-up shirt. His dark good looks caught the eye of more than one passing female and she knew it wouldn't be long before he found someone else and forgot all about her.

The thought tore at her heartstrings and to her horror, tears filled her eyes. Sierra rapidly blinked them back, glad Carl and Rachel were too engrossed in discussing the role of "shepherding" within a congregation to notice.

But she wasn't so lucky with Matt. His gaze had barely left her face since she'd sat down.

"I'd like you to come back to my office with me for a second," Matt said. "I have some papers I want you to see."

Carl shifted his gaze momentarily from Rachel. "The food should be here any minute."

"We won't be long," Matt said, pushing back his chair, rising to his feet and holding out a hand to Sierra.

She hesitated for only a second before taking the hand he offered. But the minute his skin touched hers, all the old feelings came rushing back and Sierra wondered if it was smart to be alone with him.

His hand cupped her elbow as they walked the few short blocks to his office. He kept the conversation flowing about inconsequential things and she found herself relaxing. Until they were in his outer office and he turned to face her.

"I've missed you," he said suddenly.

"Matt, please don't —" Her voice caught and she stopped, cleared her throat and started again. "Don't make this harder on both of us than it already is."

He leaned back against the door leading to his office, making no move to open it. "I love you, Sierra. I've loved you for a long time."

Her heart twisted. "Don't confuse what you felt for me with love."

"I'm not confused," he said. "I know what I feel. And I think you love me, too."

Sierra could no more deny that fact than she could deny her own name. "I do love you," she said. "But it doesn't matter. We both know that sometimes love isn't enough."

"And sometimes it is," Matt said. To her surprise he turned and unlocked his office door, pushing it open. "Come in. I want to show you something."

Sierra entered the room and stopped short, her eyes widening in surprise. She stared for a long moment before shifting her gaze back to him. "It's the hope chest from the Praise Festival."

He nodded. "I won the raffle. I want you to have it. I want you to fill it with not only linens and cooking supplies, but with your hopes and dreams."

"So my husband can one day make them come true?" Sierra scoffed, feeling her cheeks warm. "I told you I don't believe in such nonsense."

"It's not nonsense," Matt insisted. "I can make your dreams come true, if you just give me the chance."

Didn't he realize what he was doing to her? Sierra drew a ragged breath. "Matt, there are —"

"Don't give me your answer yet" he said. "Open it first. Your birthday gift is inside."

Sierra paused.

"Open it, Sierra. Please."

Reluctantly Sierra stepped forward. The cherry wood finish gleamed like satin and the chest was even more beautiful than she remembered. She crouched down and lifted the lid. There weren't any brightly wrapped gifts inside, only several pieces of paper. She shot Matt a questioning gaze.

He smiled. "I told you I had some papers I wanted you to see."

"The papers are the gift?"

He nodded.

Her fingers closed around the thin sheets and pulled them out. For a moment she couldn't figure out what they were until she realized they were crayon drawings.

"These are Maddie's," she said, recognizing the tiny lopsided hearts her daughter always drew on her pages. "How did you get them?"

"Libby brought her to the office a couple of times," Matt said nonchalantly. "And I watched her one time when Libby had to run an errand."

"You and Maddie?" Despite her best efforts to control it, Sierra's voice rose.

"I took good care of her," Matt said quickly in a reassuring tone. "She's a wonderful girl. To know her is to love her. Any man would be lucky to have such a daughter."

His words took her breath away and her heart skipped a beat. "What are you saying?"

"Look at the picture," Matt said gently.

Sierra dropped her gaze back to the paper in her hand.

"I had Maddie draw what she wanted more than anything in the world," he said. "I thought maybe she'd draw a bike or a doll, but she surprised me."

Sierra stared at the colorful drawing. "It's a house."

"And a lawn." Matt pointed to a patch of green spikes. "And that black blob is a dog."

Sierra smiled. "She's always wanted a Scottie."

"And that's you," Matt said, gesturing to a stick woman with bright yellow hair.

"Who's this?" Sierra's finger stopped on another stick figure.

"That's a dad," Matt said. "Maddie wants a house with a yard and a dog and a mom and dad. That's all she wants — just the basics."

Sierra blinked back the tears that were threatening to fall. "Once I get through school, I'm going to try to get a house for us. Then we can get a dog."

Matt gently took her hand.

"But you won't have a husband. And Maddie won't have a father. I love you, Sierra. I want to marry you. And I want to make not only your hopes and dreams come true, but Maddie's hopes and dreams, too."

Blood coursed through Sierra like an awakened river, but she held tight to her common sense. She couldn't let herself be swept away. "You said you didn't want to raise someone else's child."

"I believe I also said I wasn't ready for love and marriage," he said with a wry smile. "But that was before I fell in love with you. And Maddie won't be my stepchild, she'll be *my* child."

Though Sierra hesitated, her heart was already starting to sing. "Are you sure you have enough love for two?"

Matt laughed and pulled her into his arms. "For two and for many, many more. Just give me the chance to prove it."

Sierra wrapped her arms around his neck and raised her lips for his kiss. And, as his mouth closed over hers, she thanked God for giving her *and* Maddie the man of their dreams.

Epilogue

The outdoor dining area of the café on State Street was nearly empty. The lunch crowd had thinned to a few stragglers like Libby and Sierra who sat in the warmth of the mid-afternoon sun sipping tea and talking.

"I heard Jerry's getting married again," Libby said. "I saw his mother at the store last week."

"They say third time's a charm." Sierra lifted one shoulder in a slight shrug. "Supposedly he's turned over a new leaf. Again."

"Did you know about the marriage?"

Sierra shook her head. "We don't talk. I may have forgiven him, but it's not like we're best friends or anything."

Libby nodded understandingly and dumped a packet of sugar into her tea. "By the way, I saw Rachel at the Farmer's Market last Saturday and she told me she and Carl are expecting."

"Again?" Sierra's eyes widened. "Little Amy isn't even one."

"Rachel's going to be busy. And she's not the only one." Libby took a deep breath. "I had my ultrasound yesterday."

Sierra leaned forward. "How did it go?"

She and Libby had found out they were pregnant at the same time but, unlike Sierra and Matt who'd already found out they were having another boy, Libby and Carson were adamant they didn't want to know their baby's sex.

"You'll never believe it." Libby chuckled and her smile widened. "Dr. Lew was doing the ultrasound and all of a sudden he says to us, what do you see? Of course, I reminded him that we didn't want to know the sex but he says, 'I'm not talking about the sex, I'm talking about there being *two* babies.'"

Sierra plopped her glass on the table with such force, tea sloshed over the side and onto the tabletop. "You're having twins?"

Libby laughed. "Can you believe it? I thought Carson was going to faint."

"But he's happy about it, right?" Sierra asked, remembering how Carson had wanted to wait until his business was more established before starting a family. After opening his third restaurant this year, they'd decided the time was right and

Libby had promptly gotten pregnant.

"Ecstatic," Libby said, her lips curving up in a smile.

"Boys? Or girls?" Sierra asked.

"They're going to be fraternal," Libby said. "So it could be one of each."

"You still don't know?" Sierra asked in disbelief.

"What can I say?" Libby wrinkled her nose. "We like surprises."

"I have enough surprises in my life with an eight-year-old and a three-year-old," Sierra said with a laugh. "My motto is Be Prepared."

"I can't believe you're having another," Libby said. "You're going to be so busy."

"Thankfully Matt is great with the kids," Sierra said. "I don't know why he was so worried. He's a natural-born father."

The words had barely left her lips when Sierra saw him, the father of her children, the man who had done as he'd promised and made all her hopes and dreams come true.

He was across the street, standing in front of the Creamery with Maddie and Caleb. Each child held a large double-dip cone.

Even as she shook her head at the fool-ishness of getting each child so much ice cream, Caleb bent to look at something on the sidewalk and the entire top of his cone crashed to the ground. The boy shrieked and immediately began to wail.

Sierra started to rise but Libby put a restraining hand on her arm.

"Let him handle it," Libby said. "Live And Learn is my motto."

Matt immediately scooped his son up in his arms.

"Watch out, Daddy. Caleb's got chocolate on his hands." Maddie's voice rang loud and clear across the street and Sierra understood why Dottie thought Maddie would be a great actress. With her set of lungs, Maddie could definitely reach the back row of any theater.

The warning had barely left the girl's lips when Caleb flung his arms around his father's neck, his chubby fingers smearing chocolate ice cream across the back of Matt's new shirt.

Libby gasped.

Maddie giggled.

Sierra's breath caught in her throat.

Matt twisted around in a vain attempt to inspect the damage before he burst into laughter. He reached down and took Maddie's hand, while Caleb remained in his arms, one sticky hand looped around his neck.

"He's not even upset." A hint of awe filled Libby's tone.

"Oh, when he gets a good look at that shirt he'll probably be a little upset," Sierra said with a laugh. "But Matt understands kids and he doesn't sweat the small stuff."

Libby shook her head. "Lucky kids."

Though Sierra didn't correct her friend, she knew God had more to do with it than luck. And she would forever give Him thanks and praise for sending her a man that not only had love enough in his heart for two, but for many, many more.

Dear Reader,

Sierra Summers has a special talent; she can oink like a pig. Her friend Libby can squawk like a chicken. How about you? Me, I do a great parrot imitation. When I was on my first date with my husband, I did my parrot sound and he was really impressed. Well, at least he called for another date. One of the biggest challenges for writers is making their characters "come alive." You can't have perfect characters, because people aren't perfect; we do goofy things, sometimes we even do the wrong thing. We struggle with temptation and with our faith.

When you read the book, I hope you'll see a little of yourself in the pages. And I hope you'll discover in your own life, as Sierra did in hers, that with God, nothing is impossible.

Blessings,

Cynthia Rutledge